ODYSSEUS

The Complete Adventures

Homer

ODYSSEUS

The Complete Adventures

D. J. Hartzell

The Independent School Press

WELLESLEY HILLS
MASSACHUSETTS

All the illustrations are reproduced courtesy of
The Boston Museum of Fine Arts

PRINTED IN THE UNITED STATES OF AMERICA.

0–88334–110–7

8586
5678901

To

Joe Notterman,

A man both wise and good.

Contents

List of Illustrations

Introduction

As far as we know, the Greek poet Homer lived in the eighth century B.C. Tradition says that he was blind. Tradition also says that he was the author of two long poems, the ILIAD and the ODYSSEY. The ILIAD, generally thought to have been composed first, tells of the actions of the Greek and Trojan warriors (including Odysseus) in the tenth year of the Trojan War. The ODYSSEY relates the adventures of Odysseus during the ten years following the fall of Troy. This book is an attempt to present the *complete* story of Odysseus. Relevant material from Homer's two poems and from appropriate non-Homeric sources has been abridged and synthesized. An effort has been made to include whatever seemed of interest and whatever contributed to a consistent portrayal of a complex character, as well as to preserve the mood and tone of Homer's work without being restrained by the demands of literal translation. Like all epic poets, Homer hearkened to a by-gone age of heroic proportions in which men were grander, braver, and more fluent than the men he saw around him. My hope is that this book not only presents the particulars of Odysseus' career but also conveys the sense and flavor of the world Homer created for his hero.

The art and literature of our culture are saturated with references to the civilization of the Greeks. An excellent way to begin to understand our age is to begin to appreciate the legacy of Greece. A familiarity with the mythology of the Greeks remains essential to every student's education. Perhaps more important than their academic value is the pleasure and excitement that the stories of Greek mythology can generate. Certainly Homer was an extraordinary poet, but first of all he was a story-teller, a man who could spin a good yarn. Students in my Mythology courses are shocked to discover that the stories of gods and goddesses, heroes and heroines, are actually *enjoyable*. While they may not be ready to read Homer, they are ready and eager to learn about Zeus and Achilles, about Helen of Troy, and of course about Odysseus.

I hope anyone reading these pages will discover as much fascination as I discovered in writing them.

Dennis J. Hartzell

Jan. 1978

ODYSSEUS

The Complete Adventures

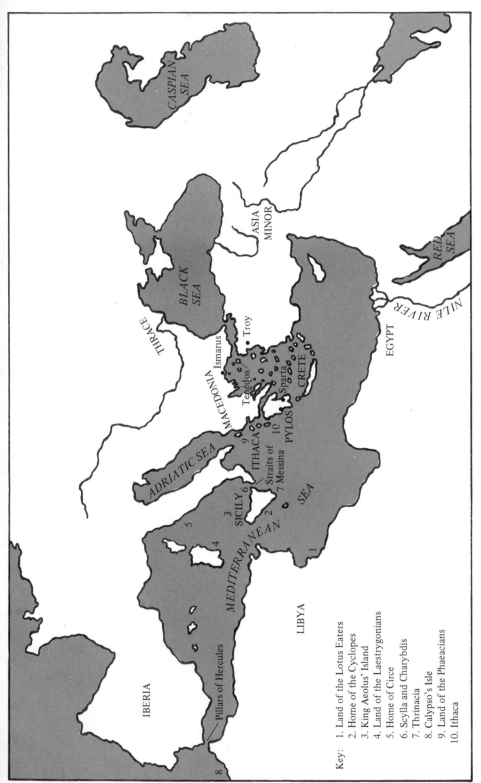

The Mediterranean Basin

Key:
1. Land of the Lotus Eaters
2. Home of the Cyclopes
3. King Aeolus' Island
4. Land of the Laestrygonians
5. Home of Circe
6. Scylla and Charybdis
7. Thrinacia
8. Calypso's Isle
9. Land of the Phaeacians
10. Ithaca

Part I

Before the Fall of Troy

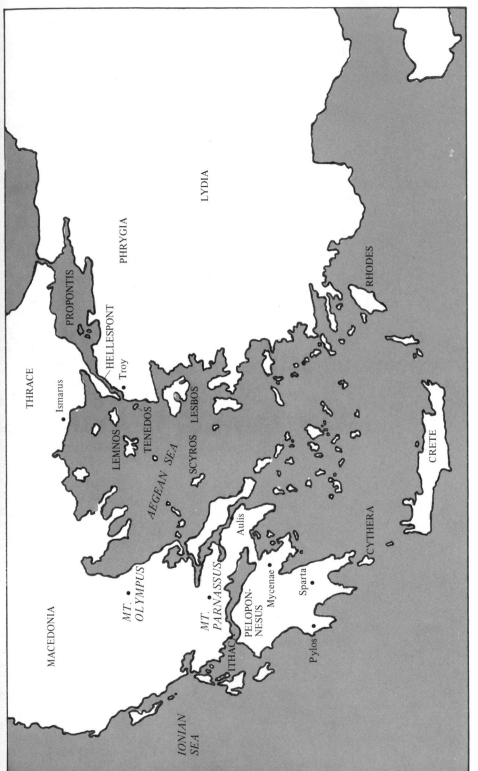

The Aegean Area

Chapter *I*

Odysseus Before the Trojan War

Approximately 3500 years ago, a great hero named Laertes was the king of Ithaca, an island kingdom off the western coast of the Greek mainland. Laertes' wife was named Anticleia, and she bore to the king a son. Shortly after the boy was born, his maternal grandfather, Autolycus, came to visit Ithaca and see his new grandson.

Autolycus was known throughout the ancient world for his cunning and craftiness. He was a son of the god Hermes (the Olympic messenger and patron god of businessmen and thieves) and the god had given certain powers to him. It was said that he could alter the color and shape of animals. He could also make objects invisible by touching them with his hands. Autolycus was not above a little sharp practice and thievery, and he had been the cause of much trouble for many men.

When Autolycus arrived in Ithaca, his infant grandson was placed in his lap. Eurycleia, the child's nurse, asked Autolycus to name the boy, hinting that a pious name meaning "a child much prayed for" would be appropriate. But Autolycus had little use for piety.

"Since I have been a man who has caused great distress to others," he said roguishly, "let the child be called 'Odysseus,' which means that he will be a man of much trouble, to himself and to his enemies."

So the son of Laertes was named, and Autolycus' prediction of Odysseus' character and life was to prove quite accurate.

Years later, when Odysseus had grown to be an adolescent, he went to visit his grandfather. Autolycus lived with his sons near

1

Mount Parnassus on the Greek mainland. They all went out to hunt a huge boar which lived in the forests around the mountain. The boar was very fierce and when the hunters approached, the animal charged. Odysseus was anxious to prove his bravery and skill, so he leaped ahead of the others to meet the beast. The boar drove straight at Odysseus and inflicted a severe wound on his thigh. The gleaming tusk pierced deep into the flesh but missed the bone. Before Odysseus fell, however, he struck the boar expertly with his spear and the animal fell roaring in the dust. Autolycus and his sons rushed forward, and while they bandaged the wounded leg they admired and congratulated Odysseus on his valor and strength. The wound healed and Odysseus returned to his home on Ithaca. But for the rest of his life he carried a great scar on his thigh. This scar would not be simply a token of Odysseus' first great deed. Later in his life it would serve an important function as a mark of identification.

Odysseus grew up to be a splendid young man. Laertes, although he was still robust and active, recognized his son's extraordinary abilities and gave him the responsibility of running the kingdom. Odysseus became King of Ithaca, and although he was a young man he quickly became known for his cleverness, his fluency, and his great ability to think while in danger. He was, like nearly all the other kings of the Greek world, a brave and accomplished warrior. But his strength of mind and his capacity to come up with shrewd solutions to difficult problems were his most notable characteristics. While the other Greek heroes most often resorted to violence and sheer physical force to achieve their goals, Odysseus most often relied on his intelligence and on the cunning he had inherited from his grandfather.

Once he became King, Odysseus decided to find a suitable woman to be his wife and Queen. All the great kings of Greece had gathered in Lacedaemon to court Helen, the step-daughter of King Tyndareus. Odysseus journeyed to Lacedaemon to join the men wooing Helen, even though he had little hope of success. Tyndareus was married to Leda, but Helen was not the daughter of their marriage. Zeus, the mightiest of all the Greek gods, was Helen's father. One day Zeus had seen Leda and fallen desperately in love with her beauty. Changing himself into a swan, Zeus raped Leda and as a result Helen was born. As we might expect from her having such a father, Helen grew up to be the loveliest woman in all the world.

Because of her extraordinary beauty, all the kings of Greece wished to marry Helen. Tyndareus found himself in a difficult position. If he gave Helen to one man, all the other heroes and warrior-kings would be angry with him; angry enough, perhaps, to attack his lands and destroy his property. So Tyndareus delayed making a decision, and the men courting Helen became more and more impatient.

Finally, Odysseus called Tyndareus aside and offered him a solution.

"King Tyndareus, I think I have a plan that will put an end to your troubles. But first you must promise me something. If my plan succeeds you must promise to use your influence to make your niece, Penelope, become my wife and the Queen of Ithaca. Agreed?"

"Agreed," replied Tyndareus.

"Then here is what you must do," said Odysseus. "Make each of the men swear an oath. Each must swear to support and defend your choice of Helen's husband. This way you are out of danger and all the kings will have sworn loyalty to the man you choose."

Tyndareus was wise enough to recognize the sense of Odysseus' plan. Each of the gathered kings swore the oath, each hoping to be the man chosen. Once he had all the kings' oaths, Tyndareus gave Helen to Menelaus, the powerful and wealthy King of Sparta.

Nor did Tyndareus forget his promise to Odysseus. When Odysseus returned to Ithaca, he brought Penelope with him as his wife. She was nearly as beautiful as Helen. She was also very talented and, appropriately, very clever.

Some time passed during which the Greek world was generally at peace. An event occurred, however, which was to lead to a most disasterous war. Many famous heroes would die in battle and one of the great cities of the ancient world would be utterly destroyed.

Located on the northwest coast of Asia Minor was the city of Troy. The king of the Trojans was Priam, a wise and just ruler who had fifty sons. One of his sons was named Paris, a young man who was very handsome but not very principled.

In a sense, Paris' choice in history's first beauty contest was the cause of the Trojan War. Eris, the goddess of discord, was angered by not being invited to the wedding of Peleus and Thetis. She made a golden apple, inscribed it with the message "For the most beautiful," and rolled it into the room where the marriage feast was being celebrated. The three most powerful Olympian goddesses each felt she deserved the apple. They were Hera, Zeus' wife and goddess of marriage; Athena, Zeus' daughter and the goddess of wisdom; and Aphrodite, goddess of love and beauty.

Zeus was thus confronted with a very difficult decision. He knew that by giving the prize to one goddess, he would antagonize the other two. The gods and goddesses on Olympus were notorious squabblers; no matter what decision Zeus made, he was sure to suffer a breach in the peace of his household. So Zeus decided that the apple should be taken to Paris (who had won a reputation for being a fair judge) and that Paris should be instructed to make the award to the goddess of his choice.

After each of the goddesses revealed herself to Paris (each trying to bribe him with promises of rewards), the Trojan prince awarded the golden apple to Aphrodite. Hera and Athena stormed off, outraged by the decision and vowing revenge on Paris and on his people. Aphrodite was properly satisfied and promised to help Paris win the love of the most beautiful woman in the world.

Shortly after this incident, which came to be known as the Judgment of Paris, Paris borrowed one of his father's ships and sailed across the Aegean Sea to visit King Menelaus of Sparta. Menelaus received Paris with great kindness and hospitality. Among the Greeks, all noble and upright men provided visitors with a generous welcome. For a month Paris enjoyed feasts and entertainment at the splendid palace in Sparta. But when Menelaus left his city for several days, Paris committed an unforgiveable crime. With the help of Aphrodite, Paris convinced Helen to elope with him to Troy. They loaded his ship with as much of Menelaus' gold as it would hold and set sail back across the Aegean Sea.

When Menelaus returned to his palace, he discovered what Paris had done and immediately notified his older brother, Agamemnon, of what had happened to Helen. Agamemnon was King of Mycenae and was recognized as the greatest and most powerful

Paris leads Helen away from the Palace of Menelaus.

5

of all the Greek kings. With Agamemnon's support, Menelaus called upon all those who had sworn to Tyndareus' oath to come to his aid and bring Helen back from Troy.

From all over the Greek world, a mighty armada began to assemble at the island of Aulis. From Aetolia came King Diomedes, a valiant and powerful warrior. From the island of Crete came the glorious Idomeneus, leading many strong followers. From Pylos came Nestor, an aged king no longer able to fight but famous for his wisdom and good advice. From Euboea came Prince Palamedes, a man well experienced in the practice of war. All those who had sworn allegiance to Menelaus brought their armies on board ship to the island of Aulis.

All except one. Odysseus did not immediately answer the call to arms. Penelope had just recently borne him a son, who was named Telemachus, and Odysseus was reluctant to leave his beloved island and his new family. In addition, the prophet Halitherses warned Odysseus that if he went to fight at Troy he would not return for twenty years.

The chieftains who had gathered at Aulis realized that they needed Odysseus' assistance if their expedition was to succeed. The city of Troy was quite powerful, with walls that were said to be impregnable, and the Trojans were fierce and accomplished warriors. The Greeks needed all the strength they could muster.

Agamemnon sent a legation to Ithaca, led by Menelaus and Palamedes. When Odysseus learned that the two kings had landed on his island, he planned to trick them. By pretending to be insane, Odysseus hoped that he could avoid having to join the expedition to Troy.

Menelaus and Palamedes arrived at the palace and discovered tht Odysseus was out in the fields. He had yoked an ox and an ass together and was plowing the field and sowing the furrows with salt, something only a madman would do.

Palamedes was well-aware of Odysseus' cleverness and was not convinced that Odysseus was truly insane. So Palamedes grabbed the infant Telemachus and placed the baby in front of the plough. When Odysseus stopped the plough to save his son, Palamedes and Menelaus knew that he had his wits about him and was not in fact mad. They called upon Odysseus to fulfill his pledge and join the Greek forces.

Realizing that his trick had failed, Odysseus agreed to meet the army at Aulis. He said farewell to his young wife and his infant son and loaded twelve ships with provisions and with several hundred of the best warriors on Ithaca. They set sail for Aulis.

Some people have said that Odysseus was dishonorable and even cowardly for trying to trick Menelaus and Palamedes. But Odysseus had excellent reasons for not wanting to sail to Troy (remember the prophecy by Halitherses); once he joined the expedition, however, he committed himself completely to making it successful. In fact, he would save the expedition on at least one occasion and would finally prove to be the most effective of all the Greek warriors at Troy.

The first of Odysseus' great contributions to the Greek cause was the recruiting of the man recognized as the greatest warrior in all the world. His name was Achilles and he was the son of the sea nymph Thetis. When Thetis learned that the Greeks were preparing to attack Troy, she knew that they would want her son, who was still quite young, to fight with them. She also knew, because she was a goddess, that if Achilles went to Troy he would die there. He would win undying fame and glory fighting the Trojans, but his fate would be unavoidable.

In desperation, Thetis disguised her son as a girl and hid him among the women on the island of Scyros. The Greek chieftains gave Odysseus the task of discovering and recruiting Achilles. Their choice was a sensible one; Odysseus was by far the cleverest and most persuasive man among the Greeks.

Perhaps he had heard a rumor or perhaps he guessed what Thetis had done, but, however he knew, Odysseus sailed off to Scyros, devising a plan to find Achilles.

Once on the island, Odysseus made his way to a great hall in the palace there. In the hall were dozens of women and young girls working at various tasks of spinning and weaving. Odysseus placed a great trunk full of gifts in the middle of the hall. The trunk was filled with beautiful fabrics and richly decorated ornaments. The trunk also contained a suit of armor and several well-made spears and swords. While the women were admiring the lovely material and the brilliant jewelry, Odysseus noticed that one girl's attention was fixed on the weapons. Odysseus then sounded a false alarm, making the others believe that the island was being attacked by pirates. The young girl who had been admiring the spears and swords immediately stripped off her womanly garments and grabbing the weapons prepared to meet the attack. The young 'girl' was, of course, Achilles. Odysseus saluted him and easily persuaded him to join the Greek army. Achilles assembled his followers, glorious warriors called Myrmidons, and sailed with Odysseus to Aulis. The Greek forces were now complete.

The fleet of the Greek allies was the mightiest military force the ancient world had ever seen. Agamemnon was chosen to be Commander-in-Chief of the hundreds of ships and thousands of men. The fleet was unable to sail, however, because Artemis (goddess of the hunt and all wild creatures) had been offended by a careless remark by Agamemnon. For many days, Artemis sent unfavorable winds, locking the great armada inside the harbor. Finally, the prophet Calchas told Agamemnon that he must sacrifice his eldest daughter, Iphigenia, in order to appease the anger of Artemis. Agamemnon was heartbroken, but he knew that the survival of the expedition demanded that he obey the oracle.

Odysseus was sent to Mycenae, charged with the task of bringing Iphigenia to Aulis. He succeeded by spinning a clever story for Clytemnestra, the wife of Agamemnon, and returned to Aulis with the girl. No one is quite certain what happened next. Some say that Iphigenia was actually sacrificed. Others say that Artemis took pity on the young girl and miraculously transported her away from the altar to live among the Taurians. In any case, the winds changed and the fleet set sail for Troy.

Most of what we know about the Trojan War is found in Homer's ILIAD. Odysseus is not the central figure in the ILIAD (that honor belongs to Achilles), but he plays a crucial role in the action.

Chapter *II*

Odysseus at Troy

When the fleet arrived in the waters off the mainland of Asia Minor, near the city of Troy, Agamemnon ordered all the ships to drop anchor. He hoped that the size and strength of the Greek forces would so frighten the Trojans that they would return Helen without a fight. Agamemnon decided to send an envoy, under a flag of truce, to Troy to attempt to persuade the Trojans to relinquish Helen and avoid the violence and bloodshed of war. The mission required a man of tact, intelligence, and eloquence. The Greek kings chose Odysseus as the man to represent them; he was accompanied by Menelaus and Palamedes.

The three Greeks were allowed to enter Troy, and King Priam insured that they were given, despite the circumstances, a hospitable welcome. The Trojans were greatly impressed by the manner and speech of Odysseus, but they had been enchanted by the beauty of Helen and refused to give her back. And although they recognized the power of the Greek forces, they were confident that their well-fortified city would withstand all assaults. Odysseus and the others returned to the fleet. There was no other course for the Greeks to take. If they were to bring Helen back to Greece, they would have to fight for her. Both sides prepared themselves for the struggle that was to come.

The city of Troy had been built on a hill a short distance from the coast. When the Greek army landed on the beaches, the Trojans were waiting and a terrific battle ensued. Many brave warriors shed their blood on that first day of fighting. For several weeks the Greeks and Trojans did battle on the great plain between the coast and the city. The results were indecisive. The

Greeks were unable to break into the city, and the Trojans were unable to drive the Greeks back into the sea.

Although the Greeks had been hopeful of a quick victory, they now recognized that they must resign themselves to a long struggle. They constructed a stockade around their beached ships and attempted to lay siege to the city. To supply themselves the Greeks began to raid cities up and down the coast of Asia Minor. The raids were led by Achilles, Odysseus, and Palamedes and were generally successful. The siege itself, however, was not successful. The Trojans had powerful allies far inland who managed to keep the city supplied with food and weapons.

For nine long years the situation remained the same. The Greeks were camped outside the city unable to breach its walls. The Trojans were trapped inside the city unable to drive the Greeks away. In the tenth year of the struggle, however, matters began to change.

Agamemnon and Achilles had a terrible quarrel and Achilles, by far the greatest of all the Greeks for actual fighting, withdrew from the action. He retired to his tents by his ships and vowed not to fight again. The Greek heroes were very proud men, and both Agamemnon and Achilles felt he had been insulted by the other.

That night Zeus sent to Agamemnon a false dream advising him to muster his forces and attack Troy without Achilles. Zeus had been persuaded to do this by Thetis, Achilles' mother, who felt that her son's honor had been compromised and that Agamemnon and the Greeks should be punished for the insult to Achilles.

So in the morning, Agamemnon summoned all the other Greek kings, telling them to assemble their men and prepare for battle. When the army had gathered, Agamemnon committed a mistake in judgement that nearly proved disasterous. He decided to test the soldiers' commitment to battle.

"Comrades and countrymen," he shouted to the troops, "I have a bitter message to deliver. For nine long years we have struggled outside the great walls of Troy, as the timbers of our ships rot in the water and our spirits are betrayed by weariness. I am beginning to think that we shall never gain the victory for which we crossed the seas. It will be a thing of great shame for us

Head of Athena.

ever after, but let us pack up our ships and sail home, leaving to the Trojans the delight of victory."

So spoke Agamemnon, hoping that the men would rise up in their pride and reject his speech. Instead they gave a great shout and began a stampede for the ships. The Greek kings were dismayed and watched in horror as the army began to disintegrate before their eyes. Athena, who had been partial to the Greek cause from the beginning, saw the disaster that threatened the expedition. She encouraged Odysseus to act.

"Great Odysseus, son of Laertes," said the goddess, "will you let all you have struggled for go to waste now? Remember all the Greeks who have died here far from the lands of their fathers. Arouse yourself and speak to the men and prevent them from this shameful retreat."

Hearing the goddess speak, Odysseus did not hesitate. He rushed to Agamemnon and grabbed the royal sceptre. Circulating among the men, Odysseus appealed to their sense of honor.

"Come now, sir," Odysseus said to each man he encountered, "this cowardly behavior of yours is not proper or right. Return now to the meeting place and bring your fellows with you. Remember your pride as a Greek and as a warrior."

In this way Odysseus managed to calm the men and convince them to assemble together once again. But once everyone was again seated, a man named Thersites, a common soldier, jumped up before the assembly. Thersites was known by all the men as one who complained and cursed endlessly. He quarreled with everyone and continually spoke rudely to Achilles and Odysseus, the two heroes he hated most. He was very ugly, having a hunched back and a pointed head with scraggly hair.

"Okay, Agamemnon," screamed Thersites, "what crack-pot scheme have you come up with now to plague us? Hasn't your greed been satisfied yet? We have brought you slave women and gold from our raids. But you bring us nothing but sorrow. You can stay here if you want, but I, for one, think we should all get out of here and go home."

In an instant, Odysseus grabbed Thersites and spoke to him.

"You foul-mouthed, misbegotten wretch. You have abused a better man for the last time. If you ever again talk in this manner,

I will strip you naked and send you howling like a beast out of the camp."

And with that Odysseus began to beat Thersites with the sceptre until the miserable man began to whine and whimper and weep. The rest of the soldiers roared with laughter, pleased that Thersites had finally been silenced.

"Good old Odysseus has done many great deeds," they said to one another, "but this is surely one of the best. At last that bragging and arrogant Thersites has gotten what he has long deserved."

Odysseus then turned and spoke to the assembled Greeks.

"Friends, we have been here a long time and you have a right to be impatient. But it would be disgraceful to strive so long for something and then to give up. Remember your pledge to bring Troy to its knees. And remember that the prophets and the oracles have told us that if we endure we will finally be victorious. So, my brave and noble comrades, what is your answer? Shall we stay and fight until the city of the Trojans is in ruins at our feet?"

The entire Greek army answered Odysseus with an enormous roar of approval. The meeting dispersed as the men armed themselves for battle. A moment of great crisis was past. Odysseus, the man who had not wanted to come to Troy, had been the one to save the expedition.

For all their renewed enthusiasm, however, the Greeks met with little success. The Trojan forces were led by Hector, Priam's oldest son and a warrior second only to Achilles in strength and skill. With Achilles not in armor, the Greeks were hard-pressed. Hector raged across the field, killing many Greeks and leading his warriors to the very edge of the Greek encampment.

The Greek army was forced back inside the stockade protecting their ships. Hector seemed invincible. Unless Achilles could be convinced to re-join the fighting, the Greeks were in great peril of being pushed back into the sea. Realizing how dangerous the situation had become, Agamemnon called his chieftains together and confessed his error in offending Achilles. The kings agreed that Achilles had to be placated and that Odysseus, Great Ajax, and Phoenix (an old friend of Achilles' father) should be the ones to try to persuade Achilles to take up arms again.

The three found Achilles sitting by the tents of the Myrmidons, singing and playing on a lyre. With him was his life-long companion, Patroclus.

"Welcome, my friends," said Achilles when he noticed Odysseus and the others standing by. "Despite all my anger with the Greeks and with Agamemnon especially, I cannot fail to greet the men whom I love best. Patroclus, mix some sweet wine and prepare comfortable seating for our guests."

Patroclus heeded his friend's request and all were soon seated and supplied with wine.

"Achilles, we drink to your health," spoke Odysseus, "and salute you as the mightiest of the Greeks here at Troy. We have not come merely to drink your delicious wine but to discuss a matter of crucial importance. Hector has been furious in battle and has brought the Trojans to the very edge of our stockade. I doubt that we can prevent him from burning our black ships unless you help us. Agamemnon confesses that he has greatly wronged you, and he swears that some god must have led his wits astray. He is now prepared to make amends by offering you splendid gifts: gold and fast horses and excellent serving women. No man would be considered poor with all the possessions which Agamemnon wishes to give to you.

"And besides, great Achilles," continued Odysseus, "do you feel no obligation to your companions and to the honor of the father who raised you? Even if your hatred for Agamemnon is unbounded, have pity on your comrades and the men who have fought beside you in the past. Surely you do not wish men in future ages to say that Hector slaughtered the Greeks and burned their ships while Achilles, the son of glorious Peleus, sat idly by."

Odysseus finished speaking and waited for mighty Achilles to answer.

"Odysseus, you have been my friend for a long time but I must answer you in the only way I can," replied Achilles. "Agamemnon has insulted my honor and I will not now fight to save his ships. And do not think that I am afraid of Hector, great though he is. I have driven him from the battlefield and into his city once before and could do so again. I will not fight, however, to save Agamemnon. Let him who has so offended me save the

Greeks from the assaults of furious Hector. I will fight only if the ships of the Myrmidons are threatened."

Nothing that Odysseus or the others said could persuade Achilles to change his decision. They returned to Agamemnon and the other chieftains with their sad news.

Men in desperate situations seek desperate solutions. The Greeks had been battered badly in the fierce fighting of recent days. The Trojans were full of the confidence that drives men on to glorious deeds. With their champion, Achilles, stubborn in his refusal to fight, the Greeks decided on a daring manuever to startle the Trojans and to renew their own spirits.

Diomedes, King of Aetolia, offered to lead a raid behind Trojan lines. Agamemnon applauded his courage.

"Diomedes, you bring delight to my heart," said Agamemnon. "But pick a comrade to accompany you on your mission, and be sure to choose that man who will not fail you in daring and valor."

"How can I hesitate to choose," replied Diomedes, "when the ideal man stands here at hand. I ask noble Odysseus to join me, and together I am sure we can survive any threat. The goddess Athena loves him above all others and he is by far the cleverest of the Greeks."

"Be careful in your praise," replied Odysseus modestly and with good humor, "for these men have known me for many years. But let us be off. The night is well advanced and we must catch the Trojans by surprise."

So the two men armed themselves, Odysseus taking up his bow and quiver and fitting a leather helmet studded with boar's teeth on his head. This helmet had once belonged to Odysseus' grandfather, Autolycus, who had long ago stolen it. Diomedes strapped on a two-edged sword and pulled over his head a skull-cap of bull's hide.

As the two made their way in the darkness, the bright-eyed Athena sent them a favorable portent in the form of a sacred heron. The heroes recognized that the goddess was with them.

"O glorious daughter of Zeus," prayed Odysseus, "stand beside me now as you have done in the past and help me to win glory among my people and to bring grief to the Trojans."

Diomedes and Odysseus moved like shadows through the darkness. As they approached the Trojan encampment, they surprised and captured a Trojan named Dolon. Hector had sent him to spy on the Greeks in their tents. By questioning Dolon, Odysseus learned that King Rhesus of Thrace had that day arrived to aid the Trojans. He had brought with him beautiful white horses whose speed was that of the wind. These horses were special for another reason as well. An oracle had prophesied that Troy would survive if the horses of King Rhesus drank the waters of a near-by river. Odysseus and Diomedes understood how important it was that these horses never approach that river.

When Dolon had told all he knew, Diomedes killed him with a single stroke of the sword. It was a brutal act, but Odysseus (and Athena) recognized its necessity. The two Greeks knew they were in no position to take prisoners for ransom.

Under cover of darkness, Odysseus and Diomedes crept into the camp of King Rhesus. The Thracians were sleeping in exhaustion from their long journey. While Odysseus silently rounded up the magnificent horses and harnessed them to a chariot, Diomedes made terrible use of his sword. In all Diomedes slaughtered thirteen men, including King Rhesus, before a whistled signal from Odysseus caused him to leave his bloody work. The two Greeks leaped aboard the chariot and rushed off into the night behind the thundering horses. Several of the survivors in the Thracian camp awakened at the sound and discovered the grisly sight of their dead companions. As Diomedes and Odysseus swept back into the Greek camp, sounds of wailing sorrow arose over the Trojan tents.

Although the daring raid had been a complete success, the Greeks suffered renewed hardship on the following day. Hector led the assault on the stockade and succeeded in smashing open its gates. The Trojans rushed through and began to attack and burn the ships. It appeared that all was lost for the Greeks.

Patroclus was unable, however, to watch his friends be defeated. He borrowed the glorious armor of Achilles and led the Myrmidons into the raging battle by the ships. The Trojans, seeing Achilles' armor, assumed that the invincible warrior had returned to the fight. They began to retreat from the Greek ships in panic. Led by Patroclus, the Myrmidons turned the Trojan retreat into a disorderly rout.

At last, beneath the very walls of Troy, Patroclus encountered Hector. Achilles had warned Patroclus to avoid Hector and to return to the ships as soon as the Trojans had been driven off. Patroclus, however, was filled with the exultation of his success and rushed to meet the Trojan hero. After a terrific struggle, Hector killed Patroclus; the Greeks then fought furiously to save Patroclus' body and carry it back to Achilles.

The death of Patroclus drove Achilles into a fit of overwhelming grief and rage. He wept and tore his hair. He threw himself upon the ground and covered his shining body with dust and filth and grime. He raised his cries of lamentation for his dead comrade to the heavens. And he swore that he would seek and win revenge; he swore that he would kill Hector.

What Odysseus had failed to do with all his persuasion, Hector had done by slaying Patroclus. Achilles was nearly mad to begin fighting. Odysseus approached him and spoke gently.

"Great Achilles, be patient and bring your sorrow under control. Night is falling, the time for all battles to halt. The men are exhausted and hungry from the long day's struggle. After a good sleep and a strengthening breakfast, we will all join you in your search for revenge."

As always, Odysseus' words were sensible and well-spoken. But Achilles refused to be consoled.

"Let the others sleep and feed if they must," he cried, "but I cannot. I will spend the hours until dawn fasting and grieving for the death of the man I have loved since I was a child."

When morning came and Aurora, goddess of the dawn, splashed the eastern skies with the colors of a new day, the Greek army arose and ate breakfast. Achilles grimly armed himself in the most remarkable armor the world had ever seen. (It had been made for him during the night by the god Hephaestus.) The Greeks marched off to battle.

Achilles' deeds on that day were astounding: countless Trojans fell before his spear and sword. And as King Priam and his Queen, Hecuba, looked on from the walls of Troy, Achilles killed Hector. His desire for revenge still not satisfied, Achilles than acted very ignobly. He tied Hector's dead body to the back of his chariot and dragged it around the walls of the city and back across the plain to the Greek camp, where he slit the throats of 13 Trojan captives. Later, Achilles would regret this behavior and return the body of Hector to Priam for a proper funeral. Not long after Hector's death, Achilles was killed, as had been foretold, by an arrow from the bow of Paris.

Before Achilles was killed, he organized a splendid funeral for his slain comrade. As was customary on such occasions, Achilles offered rich prizes to those who excelled in the athletic contests held to honor the memory of the dead. For the Greeks, life in the world was of ultimate and transcendent importance. The spectre of a shadowy, insubstantial afterlife in the house of Hades filled them with terror and dread. Thus, they cultivated an enormous appetite and energy for life. It was fitting, therefore, to commemorate a fallen comrade by celebrating, in athletic games, the powers of the body.

Odysseus entered two contests: the wrestling and the foot race. Other competitions were held in chariot racing, boxing, archery, armed combat, and spear-throwing. Odysseus' opponent in wrestling was Great Ajax, an enormous man with a rash temper who was considered second in strength only to Achilles. Odysseus and Great Ajax locked themselves together, and the watching Greeks were stunned to silence as they saw muscles and tendons swell and stretch. They could hear groans of supreme effort escape each man's lips. Being much smaller than Ajax, Odysseus seemed to have little hope of victory. Ajax's limbs and trunk were enormous and his hands exerted crushing force. But Odysseus never relied solely on brute power. Executing a series of clever moves which employed leverage and balance rather than mere strength, Odysseus threw Ajax twice to the ground. As they prepared for a third fall, Ajax was becoming violently disturbed. Rather than risk continuing the struggle, Achilles diplomatically suggested that the match be declared a draw. Although he had thrown Ajax twice, Odysseus graciously accepted Achilles' suggestion, and he and Ajax divided the prizes evenly.

In the foot race, Odysseus competed against a man from Locria known as Little Ajax (no relation to the man Odysseus had wrestled) and against Nestor's son, the swift Antilochus. Both were much younger than Odysseus and again it seemed that Odys-

Achilles drags the body of Hector around the Walls of Troy.

19

seus would have little chance of victory. But as the race neared its end, with Odysseus and Little Ajax running neck and neck, Odysseus said a silent prayer to Athena.

"Be kind, goddess of the gray eyes, and bring strength to my legs."

Athena did better than that. As the two runners approached the finish, the goddess caused Little Ajax to stumble and fall into a pile of cow dung. Odysseus crossed the line first and turned to see his opponent rise to his feet.

"I should have known," mumbled Little Ajax, spitting manure, "that Athena would never allow me to win. I'm sure she was responsible for my fall. She watches over and takes care of Odysseus as if she were his own mother."

While the Greeks were thus celebrating the funeral of Patroclus the Trojans were mourning for the death of their hero, Hector. For many days the two armies put away their thirst for battle in order to properly observe the passing of the two warriors.

Achilles seemed to have known that his personal fate decreed that his death would follow shortly after Hector's. Nonetheless, Achilles threw himself back into battle after Patroclus' funeral. He fell outside the walls of Troy, struck from a distance by an arrow shot by the cowardly Paris. (Paris himself would die from a poisoned arrow shot by a Greek named Philoctetes.)

When the dying body of Achilles crashed to the ground, a savage fight ensued over the corpse and its glorious armor. Great Ajax and Odysseus stood over the body and fought desperately to save it from being captured. Finally, Ajax lifted the corpse to his shoulders and carried it back to the Greek camp. Single-handedly, Odysseus withstood the Trojan army and protected Ajax's retreat.

After the funeral for Achilles, at which even gods and goddesses were seen to weep, the Greek kings decided to give the immortal armor of Achilles to the most deserving man. The obvious choices were Great Ajax and Odysseus, the men who had risked their lives to protect the body of their fallen comrade. A bitter argument arose between those who favored Ajax and those who favored Odysseus. The Trojans, ironically, provided the solution.

Two Greek spies returned from Troy to report their findings. They said that they had overheard theTrojans say that the man they most feared among the Greeks was Odysseus. Hearing this, the army immediately voted to give the armor to Odysseus. Ajax felt so offended by this decision that he went temporarily insane. He slaughtered a great herd of sheep, thinking they were Agmemnon, Odysseus, and others. As he killed the animals, he called them by the names of the Greek leaders. The army watched in amazement. When Ajax recovered his senses and realized what he had done, he immediately killed himself for shame. Odysseus then gave the armor to Neoptolemus, the young son of Achilles who arrived at Troy after his father's death.

It had been over nine years since the Greeks had landed at Troy. Achilles was dead. Hector was dead. The Trojans were still inside the massive walls of their city. The Greeks remained encamped by their ships. The years of fighting and violence had gotten the Greeks nowhere. The city they had sworn to destroy remained standing.

But what nearly ten years of force and battle couldn't accomplish, Odysseus accomplished by devising a masterly and daring strategem.

The best carpenter in the Greek camp was a man named Epeus. Odysseus instructed him to build an enormous wooden horse, hollow inside, with a trap-door concealed behind one of the horse's flanks. When Epeus had constructed the huge horse, Odysseus spoke to the Greek chieftains.

"Here is my plan," he said. "Two dozen or so of our bravest warriors will hide inside the horse. On a dark night, the horse will be left outside the gates of Troy. The rest of the army will break camp and board the ships and pretend to sail away. But the fleet will drop anchor on the far side of the island of Tenedos, four miles from here, where our ships will be hidden from the Trojans on shore. I will arrange that the Trojans will convey the horse into their city. When darkness falls again, we will sneak out of the horse and open the gates to the city. Under cover of night, the fleet can sail back and the army will be able to enter the city. The plan is not without risks, but it is the only way I can think of to get us inside the walls of Troy."

The Greek kings accepted the plan and, despite the peril, Odysseus had little trouble recruiting warriors to join him inside the horse. (Epeus was an exception. He was a miserable coward but was the only man who knew how to operate the secret trap-door. The others forced him to join them.)

Odysseus recognized that the major problem would be to convince the Trojans to drag the horse into the city. Among the Greeks was a man named Sinon, who was said to be very clever and a most plausible liar. Odysseus coached Sinon with great care until he was satisfied that Sinon would not fail in his instructions. Whether or not the Trojans would take in the horse would depend on Sinon's ability to lie.

On a black night, the Greeks silently moved the horse, with Odysseus and the other armed warriors inside, in front of the main gates of the city. They then loaded their ships and set fire to their tents and huts. They moved offshore to the far side of the island of Tenedos. On the ramparts of Troy, the Trojans were puzzled by the great fire blazing in their enemy's camp. The night was very dark, however, and the look-outs could see nothing.

When dawn arose, the Trojans were faced with an astonishing sight. An enormous, wooden horse stood outside their gates. The Greek camp was a smoldering ruin. The Greek fleet was nowhere to be seen. People poured out of the city to stare in wonder at the horse and to survey with growing exultation the smoking remains of the Greek camp. It was clear to them: the Greeks had given up the struggle and sailed home. The war was over at last.

Many Trojans were puzzled and a little frightened by the horse. A debate arose between those who wished to destroy it and those who wished to bring it into the city. Cassandra, one of Priam's daughters, insisted that the horse be destroyed. But Cassandra has been both blessed and cursed by Apollo, the god of prophecy. She always saw and spoke the truth (quite a blessing), but no one ever believed her (quite a curse). The Trojans ignored Cassandra's warnings.

A son of Priam's named Laocoon stepped forward.

"I suspect and fear the Greeks even when they leave gifts," said Laocoon. "The horse must be burned."

At this point, Sinon was brought before Priam. He had been captured near the Greek camp.

"You are a Greek, are you not?" asked Priam.

"Yes sir, I am, but I swear to the gods that I wish I were not," replied Sinon.

"Where is your army?" Priam asked.

"They have sailed home to Greece." Sinon had learned his story well. "They were going to sacrifice me as an offering to the gods but I managed to escape and hide. I hope they all die at sea before they can return to their homes and families."

"And what of this horse? Why have the Greeks left it outside our gates? And speak truthfully," continued Priam, "if you wish to see another dawn."

"Noble sir," said Sinon, "I now hate the Greeks as I once hated the Trojans. Agamemnon was going to kill me on the altar. You may be sure that I would do anything to bring grief upon them. The horse, good sir, was built as a sacred offering to the goddess Athena. The Greeks left it here hoping you would destroy it and thus bring down the anger of the goddess upon your city. The truth is, however, that your people will be regarded with great favor by the goddess if you move the horse to a place of honor inside your city."

Priam was nearly convinced by Sinon's story.

"The man is lying," cried Laocoon. "King Priam, do not believe this slippery, sharp-eyed Greek. I say we must destroy the horse."

At that moment, two giant sea serpents rose from the waves and slithered across the plain. They had been sent by Athena, who wished Odysseus' plan to succeed. The monsters coiled around Laocoon and his two sons and crushed them to death. They then returned to the sea.

When the Trojans recovered from their speechless horror, all agreed that Sinon must have told the truth and that Laocoon had been punished for disbelieving the story. Priam ordered his people to drag the horse into the city.

"Incidentally, Sinon," said Priam, "why is the horse so large?"

"Another clever idea of that rascal Odysseus," replied Sinon. "He hoped that when you saw the size of the horse you would destroy it rather than take the trouble of dragging it inside Troy's formidable walls."

Priam was satisfied. The Trojans moved the horse to the center of the city. Odysseus' plan was working perfectly.

All that day and into the evening, the city of Troy was the scene of great celebration. After long years of struggle, privation, and death, the war had ended. When darkness fell, the Trojans retired to their beds exhausted but very happy. For the first time in nearly ten years they posted no watchmen or sentries.

Throughout the day, Odysseus and his comrades had remained still and silent inside the horse. Each man conquered his uncertainty and fear in his own way. Only Epeus broke under the pressure and began to whine in terror.

"Be quiet, you miserable coward," hissed Odysseus in a low whisper. "The next sound you make will be your last."

Being more afraid of Odysseus than of the Trojans, Epeus nursed his fear in silence.

When Odysseus heard the sounds of celebration and merry-making die down in the city, he motioned to the others.

"My friends, the time has come. Epeus, open the trap-door. And may Athena, the radiant daughter of Zeus, sustain our courage and strength."

One by one the Greeks dropped down from the horse. Troy and its people slept unsuspecting around them. Odysseus crept to the great gates and threw them open. The Greek army was waiting. They had returned to shore by rowing with muffled oars.

Through the opened gates streamed the Greeks, raising their terrible battle cry. The Trojans were taken completely by surprise. Many of their brave warriors were cut down in their beds. Others, however, managed to arm themselves and offer resistance. The fighting was brutal. From street to street and house to house, the Trojans fought with the desperation of cornered animals. Each Trojan wished to sell his life as dearly as possible, killing as many Greeks as he could before he died. The Greeks lost many men, but the element of surprise had crippled the Trojans and the end was inevitable.

Hecuba throws out her arms in horror as Neoptolemus prepares to plunge his sword into aged Priam.

25

After opening the gates, Odysseus had joined Menelaus in running straight to the house of Deiphobus, who had forced Helen to live with him after Paris' death. The fighting here was particularly savage before Menelaus killed Deiphobus and secured Helen. Neoptolemus, meanwhile, fought his way into the royal palace. To avenge the death of his father, Neoptolemus killed Priam and hurled Hector's young son off the walls of the city.

The Greek forces had been away from their homes and loved ones for nearly ten years. When they found themselves in Troy at last, they went berserk. By morning the rape of Troy was complete. What had once been one of the most splendid cities of the world was now a heap of charred and bloody ruins. The Trojan War was over.

Part II

After the Fall of Troy

The excessively violent behavior of the Greeks during the sack of Troy displeased the gods, even those who had always looked with favor upon the Greek cause. As a result, many of the Greek chieftains did not enjoy the triumphant homecoming they anticipated. When the fleet set sail for home, Zeus raised a howling storm which scattered the ships across the eastern Mediterranean. Many Greeks died beneath the raging waves. Agamemnon managed to save one ship and return to Mycenae. There he was murdered by his wife and her lover. Menelaus' ship was blown so far off-course that he wandered for eight years before returning to Sparta.

The story of what happened to Odysseus after the destruction of Troy is told by Homer's second epic poem, the ODYSSEY. Like the ILIAD, the ODYSSEY contains twenty-four books. But while the setting of the ILIAD is focused in time (the tenth year of the war) and place (the city of Troy and the Greek encampment outside the city), the setting of the ODYSSEY covers ten years and sweeps across much of the ancient world as it was known to the Greeks. Homer tells the story by using a fairly complicated series of flashbacks and narrative leaps, a method I have preserved in re-telling his tale. It is one of the great stories of all time.

Chapter *I*

The Adventures of Telemachus

In the tenth year after the destruction of Troy, the gods of Olympus sat in council. All the radiant and powerful divinities were there except for Poseidon, the god of the seas whom men called the Earthshaker. Poseidon was off visiting and feasting with the Ethiopians.

Athena arose to address Zeus, mightiest of the gods.

"Father Zeus, lord of the thunderbolt and son of Cronus, my heart and mind are greatly distressed for the sake of long-suffering Odysseus. It is now the tenth year since the Greeks sacked Priam's citadel at Troy and yet still Odysseus is prevented from returning to his home on Ithaca. The nymph Calypso detains him on her distant island and all the while Odysseus longs to see the smoke rising from the hearth-fires of Ithaca. O mighty Zeus, gatherer of clouds, how can your heart remain so hard against him? Did not wise Odysseus make you magnificent sacrifices on the plain of Troy?"

"My daughter," replied Zeus, "your words surprise me. How could I ever forget godlike Odysseus? Before all other men, he has done honor to us who hold the Olympian heights. But it is not I who restrain Odysseus from returning to Ithaca. My brother, Poseidon, has held a grudge against him since Odysseus blinded the Cyclops Polyphemus, Poseidon's son. But now I believe Poseidon shall have to put away his anger, for it is our will that Odysseus return home. I shall dispatch our messenger, Hermes, to the island of Ogygia. There he shall tell Calypso to release the resourceful Odysseus and provide him with the means to return to his wife and son."

"And I will make my way to Ithaca," said Athena, "and give

advice and confidence to Odysseus' son, Telemachus, who is grown now to be a splendid young man. His troubles are great and he will welcome my assistance."

The goddess bound immortal sandals upon her feet and descended in a flash to the island home of Odysseus. There was indeed much trouble in Ithaca. When Troy fell, Penelope waited in vain fo her husband to return home. Year followed year and neither did Odysseus come home nor did any reliable news of his fate reach his faithful wife. The young men of Ithaca and the surrounding islands of Doulichion and Same tried to convince Penelope that Odysseus was dead. Each day, for over three years, these one hundred and eight men, whom everyone called the Suitors, tried to persuade Penelope to marry one of them. They would gather daily at Odysseus' house and eat great feasts and drink much wine, wasting the wealth that Odysseus had secured for his family.

Although the Suitors were all noblemen, they behaved very badly. Even Antinous and Eurymachus, the best men among them, were rude, haughty, and arrogant. They would not accept Penelope's continued devotion to her husband, and day by day they depleted Odysseus' flocks and provisions. Telemachus was powerless, being alone and only in his twentieth year, to drive the Suitors from his home.

When Athena arrived on Ithaca, she disguised herself as an old friend of Odysseus' from across the seas. Telemachus welcomed her warmly and graciously into the palace, where she observed the shameful behavior of the Suitors.

"Sir, you are most welcome here," said Telemachus, "but I must apologize for these men you see here. They are disorderly and violent in their pursuit of my mother. If I could, I would drive them away, but you see I am but one and they are many."

"Telemachus, I have loved your father the way a man loves his own brother," said the goddess. "And now these proud and overbearing Suitors dishonor his house and his beautiful, faithful wife. If Odysseus were here, these men would not live long. This is what I think you must do, Telemachus: call together in council all the elders of Ithaca and explain your situation. If the Suitors will not listen to reason, you must take a ship and sail off to sandy

Pylos, the home of aged Nestor. Perhaps there you will find news of your father."

When Athena finished speaking, she changed into a bird and soared away. Telemachus was amazed at the sight but understood that a goddess had been with him. He went immediately to act upon her advice. When the elders (and the Suitors) had all gathered in the meeting place, Telemachus arose in anger to address them.

"Gentlemen, two evils have befallen my household. First, my father, your own king, is lost and probably dead. Second, these Suitors, whom you see here, are now destroying my wealth by their reckless and extravagant feasting. Against my mother's will they beset her with proposals of marriage. They destroy my inheritance and pester my mother beyond any sense of decency. Even you, the elders of Ithaca, must be scandalized by their actions. Help me, gentlemen, to drive the Suitors from my home so that my mother and I may cope with our sorrows alone and in peace."

For a moment everyone remained silent; no one seemed to know how to answer Telemachus. Finally, Antinous, the haughtiest of the Suitors, arose and replied in angry words.

"Telemachus, what a bunch of nonsense you have spoken against us. We are not at fault in this matter, but your mother is. For nearly four years she has denied our desires and clung to the absurd hope that Odysseus will return. And have you forgotten her last trick to put us off, a plan that would have pleased Odysseus himself? She set up a great loom in the palace and began to weave. She told us she could not marry until she had woven a shroud for the time when old Laertes, her father-in-law, finally dies. And we believed her. But each night she would unravel what she had woven by day. For three years she fooled us with this device, but we discovered her and made her finish. Yet she still denies us. Never will we leave your house until she marries one of us. And there are no men hereabouts strong enough to make us quit."

Several of the elders spoke to restrain the Suitors, but the arrogant young men answered each rudely. The assembly broke up with angry words on all sides. The Suitors returned to their feasting at the palace of Odysseus. Telemachus walked out alone along the beach, his heart full of sorrow.

Athena disguised herself as Mentor, an old friend of Odysseus' family, and met Telemachus by the waves. She told him that she was preparing a ship to take him to Nestor's home at Pylos. While Telemachus went off to secure provisions for the journey, Athena recruited the best men she could find to serve as crew for the vessel. With a freshening stern wind to aid him, Telemachus and 'Mentor' set sail for Pylos. Back at Odysseus' palace, the Suitors were enraged by Telemachus' departure, thinking that he might have gone to secure allies against them. They planned to ambush and kill Telemachus before he could return home.

Nestor had been too old to fight when he had accompanied the Greeks to Troy. Because he had not actually participated in the brutal destruction of the city, Zeus had allowed him alone of all the Greeks to return without mishap to his home.

When Telemachus arrived in Pylos, Nestor was enjoying an ever riper old age with his sons and his many possessions around him. The aged king welcomed his young guest with delight and set a sumptuous feast for him. Nestor had always been a ready if somewhat long-winded talker. Late into the night he filled Telemachus' ear with stories of Troy and the unfortunate fates of Agamemnon and Menelaus. But Nestor had no information about Odysseus.

"Telemachus, I am filled with wonder when I look upon you, so much are you like your father. And what a man your father was for shrewdness and cunning. There was no man like him. And never once did we disagree, he and I, as we plotted the ruin of Troy. But, alas, I know nothing of his fate. In the nearly ten years since my return I have not stirred from my home here in sandy Pylos." Nestor paused in thought. "Here is what I think you must do. Menelaus is but recently home from abroad. It is more likely that he will have the information you seek. When dawn arises, I will have my son, Peisistratos, take you in a chariot to the palace of glorious Menelaus. Does that suit you, my young friend?"

"No more could I ask, sir," replied Telemachus, "unless it be to ask leave to go to bed, for fatigue sits heavily upon me."

Nestor arranged a luxurious chamber for Telemachus and the household retired for the night.

In the clear light of the early morning, Telemachus and Peisistratos set off for Sparta. Their horses drove them swiftly across the plain of Lacedaemon, and as the sun began to descend the young men arrived at the magnificent palace of King Menelaus. They stared in wonder at the high ceilings, the shining walls, and the abundant wealth of a man loved by Zeus. Everywhere gleamed gold, silver, and ivory.

Menelaus welcomed the young travellers with warmth and grace and set before them a generous dinner.

"Help yourselves to food and wine," said Menelaus, "and when you have eaten and drunk your fill you may tell me who you are and what has brought you to Sparta. If there be some favor that I can do for you, be assured that you need but ask and it will be done."

The young men ate and drank with gusto. While they were enjoying their dinner, Helen entered the hall and took the seat next to her husband. The years had done nothing to dim her extraordinary beauty, and Telemachus thought that only a goddess could be so lovely.

"Dearest husband," said Helen to Menelaus, "do we know who these handsome young strangers are? Perhaps I should remain silent, but I have never seen such a likeness as this man has to great-hearted Odysseus. Can it be that this is Telemachus, the infant son whom Odysseus left to fight for my sake in windy Troy?"

So Telemachus was identified.

"Nothing could delight me more," cried Menelaus, "than to welcome the son of the man I have loved beyond all others. In my time I have seen many heroes and travelled through many lands, but never have I met a man to match the mind and heart of Odysseus. But tell me, Telemachus, what has brought you across the sea to my palace?"

Telemachus proceeded to explain his situation, and Menelaus was saddened to hear that Odysseus had not yet returned home. Menelaus himself had wandered for eight years after Troy's fall before finding his way home. The prophetic god, Proteus, called by men the Old Man of the Sea, had finally instructed Menelaus how to return to Sparta. Proteus also told Menelaus of the fate of Agamemnon and of the predicament of Odysseus, detained by Calypso on her island far from the shores of Ithaca.

"That is all I know of your father," said Menelaus. "He was being held by the nymph and spent his days weeping in despair of seeing his faithful wife."

Although Menelaus urged Telemachus to remain in Sparta for a long visit, the son of Odysseus was eager to return to his home. So Menelaus presented him with a most valuable gift and sent him with Peisistratos across the plain of Lacedaemon to Pylos. Telemachus paid his respects to the aged Nestor and rejoined his ship for the voyage back to Ithaca. Athena, still in disguise as Mentor, met him at the ship. She had learned of the Suitors' evil plot to murder Telemachus, and as they set sail she advised him how to avoid the ambush and return safely to his home.

Chapter *II*

The Wanderings of Odysseus

I.

While Athena was off assisting Telemachus in his journey to Pylos and Sparta, Zeus had not forgotten his promise to provide for Odysseus' return to Ithaca. The lord of gods and men dispatched Hermes to the island of Ogygia, where lived the nymph, Calypso. The message Hermes carried to the nymph was simple: provide Odysseus with a raft and provisions to leave Ogygia.

In a flash Hermes descended from Olympus and sped across the waters to the island of Calypso. He found the nymph in her cavern, singing sweetly and weaving on a golden loom. Close by the cave were stately and fragrant trees. Vines heavy with ripened grapes clustered around the cavern's entrance. Nearby were four fountains, each filled with sparkling water that danced in the sunlight. Meadows swaying with flowers stretched away on all sides. Accustomed though he was to the splendors of Olympus, Hermes admired with delight the scene before him.

Entering the cavern, Hermes greeted the nymph and delivered to her the message of Zeus. Calypso listened to Hermes with growing displeasure.

"Oh, you gods who dwell on Olympus are heartless. Have I not cared for this man for seven years? It was I who rescued him from the seas when all his companions had perished. Here on my lovely island far from cities and the paths of men, I have loved Odysseus and sought again and again to make him immortal and my husband. Always, however, his thoughts are of going home. No one can disobey the will of Zeus," she said sadly. "If Odysseus wishes to leave, I will detain him no longer."

35

Hermes took again to the air and Calypso went in search of Odysseus. She found him sitting on the beach, his eyes wet with tears as he gazed across the waves, longing for his home. Each night, Odysseus would sleep beside the lovely nymph; even so, his thoughts were far from her bed. Each day he would sit by the shore, never ceasing to dream of Ithaca and of his wife.

Calypso told Odysseus of Zeus' message and promised to provide him with tools to make a raft. They walked back to the cavern and sat down to dine. Calypso made one last attempt to persuade Odysseus to remain with her.

"Odysseus, are you still so eager to return to the land of your fathers? I beg you to remain here with me on my island and be lord of my household. If you knew how many more hardships await you upon the seas, you would forget your faithful wife. I offer you my island, myself, and a chance to live forever, for I have the power to make you immortal. Surely your home is not so lovely as my island. And surely your wife is not superior to me in beauty."

"Calypso, you are undoubtedly right," replied Odysseus. "Penelope cannot match your beauty since she is mortal and you are a goddess. Nor can Ithaca, a rough and rocky place, equal Ogygia in beauty. And yet nothing can make me happy except the sight of my native land and my faithful wife. I have already endured much suffering, and if I must suffer more I will gladly endure it also to return to the land of my birth. Nymph, do not be angry with me. I wish to go home."

The next day, Odysseus set to work to construct a raft. He cut down twenty trees, which he then trimmed and planed. He fit the boards expertly and fashioned a mast and a steering oar. Using cloth provided by Calypso, he stitched sails and lines. In four days the raft was completed. Odysseus stocked the craft with water and provisions to maintain his strength during the journey.

With a favoring breeze and a joyful heart, Odysseus left behind Calypso's island paradise and the goddess' offer of immortality. For seventeen days, Odysseus sailed onward without incident. On the eighteenth day after his departure from Ogygia, disaster struck. Poseidon was returning from his visit to the Ethiopians and spied Odysseus on the raft. The god of the sea was angry that Zeus had allowed Odysseus to begin his homeward journey. Poseidon knew that to disobey Zeus' will was dangerous, but he still wished to cause Odysseus trouble. (Poseidon had hated Odysseus since the Ithacan had blinded Polyphemus, one of Poseidon's sons. More about this later.) Stirring up a raging storm, Poseidon wrecked the raft and Odysseus was flung into the wind-driven waves.

With the ocean roaring and surging around him and the wind whistling above his head, Odysseus struggled to stay alive. For two days he fought the seas. Although the situation appeared hopeless, Odysseus refused to slip peacefully to oblivion beneath the waves. At last, a sea nymph named Leucothea took pity on the valiant man and assisted him to swim ashore to nearby Scheria, the land of the Phaeacians.

Odysseus dragged himself onto the beach. His plight seemed scarcely better than when he had battled the ocean's fury. He was exhausted and nearly dead from hunger and thirst. He had no idea where he was. Naked and unarmed, he knew not whether the land was inhabited by hostile men and savage beasts. As darkness began to fall Odysseus crawled wearily beneath the tangled branches of several nearby bushes. Covering himself with leaves, he fell into a deep healing slumber.

Athena was watching over Odysseus and now arranged to have him rescued. While he slept, the goddess slipped into the nearby city of the Phaeacians. Alcinous was the king of this land, and his daughter was a beautiful young princess named Nausicaa. Athena appeared to the young girl in a dream and urged her to take the family's laundry on the following morning and wash it in a stream outside the city. Athena knew that the stream ran close to where Odysseus slept.

When Nausicaa awoke, she gathered her handmaidens and all the soiled linen and left with them for the stream. The girls washed and rinsed the clothes in the sparkling water and placed them along the beach to dry. Then they enjoyed a swim and a picnic along the stream's banks. After the princess and the maidens had eaten, they began to play a game of ball. Nausicaa threw the ball beyond one of her friends, and it fell into the rushing water. All of the girls shouted aloud at this, and their cries awakened Odysseus.

Peering out from the bushes, Odysseus saw the group of girls. He was startled by the youth and beauty of Nausicaa. He tore off several leafy branches with which to conceal his manly parts and left the cover of his sleeping place. When the girls saw him, his skin and hair crusted with salt and his beard matted with brine, they scattered screaming along the beach. Only Nausicaa stood fast, encouraged by Athena. Odysseus approached, not too near, and addressed her.

"Surely you are one of the immortals, for I swear that only a goddess could be so lovely. But if you are a mortal, how proud your parents and brothers must be." Odysseus knew how to flatter and please a maiden with words. He was in a desperate condition and needed food and clothing. "Young lady, you see before you a most unfortunate, shipwrecked man. If you could provide me with some rag to wear and direct me to some town or city the gods will surely bless you for your kindness."

Nausicaa was impressed by the stranger's speech. She called her handmaidens back to her and scolded them for their timidity. She then offered Odysseus food and one of the shining garments which was newly washed and dried. When Odysseus had eaten and bathed and dressed himself, the girls stared at him in wonder. Nausicaa thought that he looked like a very god and wished silently that someday she might have a husband like this man.

"Stranger, I will now show you to the city," said Nausicaa, "and tell you how to find my father's palace. But I will not lead you through the city itself lest some prying eyes and carping tongues spread scandal about me. My father is Alcinous, king of the Phaeacians, and he will surely supply all your needs. Make certain, however, that you also impress my mother, Queen Arete, for she has great influence and power over my father."

Nausicaa led Odysseus to the outskirts of the city and parted from him in a grove of poplar trees. When he had given the discreet princess ample time to reach her home, Odysseus entered the city and made his way to the palace of King Alcinous. While he went through the city, Athena wrapped a mist about him so no one would hinder his progress. He found the King and Queen and nobles of the land concluding a feast. Without hesitation, Odysseus strode up to Queen Arete, clasped her by the knees, and

Odysseus, directed by Athena, advances to seek food and clothing from Nausicaa.

asked that she help him find his way home. In humility, Odysseus then sat down in the ashes of the hearth. But Alcinous nobly took him by the hand and brought him to a place of honor at the table. There Odysseus ate and drank his fill.

"Hear me, you members of my council," said Alcinous to the gathering, "return to my palace at dawn so that we may discuss how best to accommodate this stranger in his requests. He appears to be a respectable man and, indeed, even resembles one of the gods themselves. Until tomorrow, return to your houses and enjoy your rest."

After the others had departed, Queen Arete recognized the clothing worn by Odysseus and asked him how he had obtained it.

"Gracious queen," replied Odysseus, "my troubles would take a long time to tell. Let me just say that my ship was wrecked in a terrible storm and I nearly perished beneath the waves. I was washed up on your shores more dead than alive. When I saw your daughter, I begged her to give me clothing and assistance. She responded as any fond mother would wish her daughter to respond. She fed and clothed me and brought me to your city. Nausicaa is a child of great discretion as well as great beauty. You must be quite proud of her."

"So we are," said Alcinous. "And you are such a man as I would want for a son-in-law if you wished to stay here among the Phaeacians. But if your heart is set on your homecoming, we will arrange that in the morning."

Odysseus declined Alcinous' gracious, if somewhat hasty, offer of his daughter, and repeated his desire to be conveyed home. It was the custom among well-bred people not to ask their guests more than the guest wished to reveal of himself. Therefore, the King and Queen of the Phaeacians retired for the evening without knowing the true identity of the man they had welcomed into their home.

The next day a handsome feast was held in Odysseus' honor at the palace. The blind bard of Alcinous' court, Demodocus by name, was brought forward to entertain the gathering. Demodocus sang of the war at Troy and of the exploits of resourceful Odysseus. Remembering his slain comrades, Odysseus began to weep silently, hiding his tears behind his cloak. Alcinous noticed that his guest was discomfited by the songs and interrupted Demodocus to call for athletic contests. Although he did not know who his guest was, Alcinous was too polite to inquire the reason for the stranger's tears.

The young men of Scheria proceeded to compete in various contests. When it came time for the discus throw, the young men invited Odysseus to join them in competition. When he declined, one of the Phaeacians spoke roughly and offensively, hinting that Odysseus was a weakling ashamed of his athletic abilities. In anger, Odysseus sprang up and grabbed a heavier discus than the one the young men had been using. With ease he threw it far beyond their best mark. He then challenged any of the Phaeacians to a wrestling or boxing match. Having seen the stranger throw the discus, no one was eager to answer his challenge.

To avoid any further unpleasantness, Alcinous invited everyone to enter the palace and resume the feast. Dancers and musicians were summoned and Odysseus marvelled at their grace and skill. Demodocus was once again called upon to sing. The blind bard entertained the company with a tale about the adulterous love affair between Aphrodite and Ares.

Aphrodite, goddess of love and beauty, was the wife of Hephaestus, lame blacksmith and armorer of the gods. Hephaestus suspected that his wife had formed a liason with Ares, the god of war. In order to trap and punish the couple, Hephaestus made a net of gold that was so fine it was nearly invisible. The next time Aphrodite and Ares met, Hephaestus crept upon them and cast the net over them. He then called all the other gods to come and witness his wife's shame. Laughter rolled through the halls of Olympus as the gods saw Aphrodite and her lover caught in their compromising embrace. The embarrassment and shame felt by the couple were ample punishment for their wrongdoing. Even so, Hermes drew Apollo aside and remarked with a chuckle that Aphrodite was so lovely and desirable that he wouldn't care how many nets were thrown over him if he could once share the goddess' affections.

The Phaeacians were immensely pleased by this song and Demodocus was asked to continue. The bard began to sing of Troy and of the brilliant plan by which the Greeks had entered the city. Once again Odysseus was overcome by grief as he remembered the brave men who had died at Troy. Alcinous again noticed the tears in his guest's eyes and interrupted the song of Demodocus.

"Stranger and honored guest," said Alcinous gently, "this is the second time I have seen you try to hide your grief when the events of Troy were told. Will you now tell us the cause of your pain? We respect you as a noble and honorable man, yet we still do not know your name or your country. Favor us now, if so you are moved, and tell us who and what you are and what troubles have been yours."

Odysseus realized that his host's intentions were kind. He saw that it was time to discard his reserve and circumspection.

"Alcinous, you ask me of my sufferings. They will not be quickly told, for much have I endured in many lands and in various seas. But first you wish me to identify myself and my country. Know then that I am Odysseus, son of Laertes, acclaimed by all men for my shrewdness and cunning. My home is in sunny Ithaca, a rugged and rocky place yet a mother of good and valiant men. It is now the twentieth year since I left my wife and son to fight beside the Greeks at Troy. If you wish I will relate to you all that has befallen me since I left Priam's city in ruins ten years ago."

Alcinous and the Phaeacians were astonished when they learned the identity of their guest. They begged him to go on with his story. As everyone settled himself in his place, Odysseus began to speak. This is his story:

II.

After the destruction of Troy, Odysseus prepared his twelve black ships for the journey home. He sailed north toward Thrace and landed at the city of Ismarus, which was inhabited by a race of people called the Ciconians. Odysseus and his men sacked the city and drove off the Ciconians, winning for themselves great piles of treasure. Against Odysseus' advice the men proceeded to celebrate their victory by preparing a feast. While the Ithacans ate and drank, the Ciconians returned to their city with powerful allies. Odysseus and his men were forced to fight a fierce battle in order to escape on their ships. They lost seventy-two men in the counter-attack by the Ciconians.

Head of the Cyclops, Polyphemus.

Leaving Ismarus, the fleet was struck by storm winds and strong currents and driven south and west to the island of the Lotus-Eaters. The lotus plant produced a honey-sweet fruit which was delicious and harmless, except that anyone who tasted the fruit lost all conception of duty and responsibility. Three of Odysseus' men ate of the fruit and promptly forgot all about returning home. The three men wished to do nothing more than remain on the island and eat the lotus plant. Odysseus was forced to tie up the men and drag them back on board the ships, making sure that none of his other followers had a chance to succumb to the temptation of a dreamy, irresponsible life amongst the Lotus-Eaters.

Odysseus knew that he had lost his way, but he had no choice but to sail on. The fleet headed north and landed on an island near the western coast of the Italian Peninsula. Odysseus instructed the fleet to remain at anchor while he took a single ship to explore the mainland. Odysseus was full of curiosity about the inhabitants of the country and did not wish to sail on until he had discovered the manner of creature who lived there.

They pulled their ship high up on the beach, and Odysseus and twelve others moved inland until they discovered an enormous cave. Inside the cave they found huge baskets filled with milk and cheese. Herds of lambs and kids were penned inside fences. Odysseus and his companions helped themselves to some cheese and waited with great expectation for the master of the cave to return home. They did not have long to wait.

Odysseus did not know that he had come to the land of the Cyclopes, monstrous creatures of great size with a single eye in the center of their foreheads. The Cyclopes were savage and uncivilized. They had no laws or institutions. They lived off the natural fruits of the land without cultivating the soil, and they kept herds of wild goats and sheep. Their behavior and manners were barbaric. By far the most brutal of the Cyclopes was Polyphemus, who claimed Poseidon as his father. And it was to the cave of savage Polyphemus that Odysseus and his men had come.

The Cyclops drove his herds into his cave and rolled an enormous stone in front of the entrance. Odysseus and his companions were terrified at the sight of the monster and scattered to the corners of the cavern. When Polyphemus had milked and penned his flocks, he noticed the men in his cave.

"Who are you strangers who have invaded my home?" Polyphemus' voice boomed off the enclosed walls.

Odysseus advanced boldly. "We are warriors returning from Troy," he replied. "We have been blown off course and seek refuge and assistance from you. We ask this in the name of Zeus, who protects the rights of guests and travellers."

"You wretched little fool," roared Polyphemus, "I will show you how much I care for Zeus."

The Cyclops reached out suddenly and grabbed two of the men. He smashed their heads against the wall and then devoured them greedily. When he had finished his grisly meal, Polyphemus stretched out on the ground and was soon snoring mightily. Odysseus was tempted to wield his sword and kill the Cyclops right then. He knew, however, that to do so would mean a horrible lingering death for him and his men. Never would they be able to remove the stone from the mouth of the cave.

When morning came, Polyphemus arose and cannabalized two more of the men. Gathering his flocks and whistling loudly, he left the cave but made sure the stone was put securely in place behind him. Odysseus did not waste time. While Polyphemus had slept, Odysseus had devised a plan. He found the trunk of an olive tree lying in the cave. Together with his men he cut off a length of th log, smoothed it, and sharpened a point on one end. After they held the wood over the fire to make it hard, they hid it beneath the sheep droppings which littered the cave. Then they waited for the Cyclops to return.

Polyphemus re-entered the cavern as he had the night before, driving in his flocks and replacing the great stone. He immediately grabbed two more men and ate them. Odysseus approached him and offered a skin of wine which he had taken from the Ciconians at Ismarus. The wine was pleasing to the taste but very potent. The cyclops gulped down the wine and called for more.

"Never have I tasted such wine," said Polyphemus. "Tell me your name so that I may reward you properly for this gift."

"My name," said Odysseus, "is Nobody. That is what all my family and my companions call me."

"Well then, Nobody," the Cyclops roared, "here is your gift. I will eat you last of all. You will live longer than all your friends."

But with that Polyphemus was overcome by the wine and crashed to the ground in a drunken stupor. Odysseus and his men worked quickly. They retrieved the huge spear they had made and held its point in the fire until it glowed red-hot. They then drove the spear into the single eye of the monster. The point struck home and boiling, scorching blood erupted from the wound. Polyphemus awoke with a deafening, horrible roar. He lurched about the cave in his blind agony and called to the other Cyclopes on the island. Several of these answered his cries and asked what the matter was.

"My friends, Nobody is trying to kill me," moaned Polyphemus.

"Well, if nobody is trying to kill you," they grumbled, "why are you making such a racket and disturbing the rest of us?"

The other Cyclopes departed and Odysseus rejoiced at how his plan was working. While Polyphemus groaned and wept in pain, Odysseus busied himself by tying the sheep together in sets of three. Under each set he tied one of his men. When dawn appeared, Polyphemus rolled back the stone. As his flocks left the cave he felt carefully along their backs but neglected to feel their undersides. When Odysseus saw that his companions had gotten out, he grabbed onto the fleecy belly of the largest ram of the flock. Once outside the cave, he ran among the sheep and untied his friends. They drove the flock down to their ship and pushed off from shore. But Odysseus could not leave in silence. The thought of his butchered comrades haunted him.

"Cyclops, listen to me," shouted Odysseus from the deck of his ship, "you have been well repaid for your savagery and violence."

Polyphemus interrupted Odysseus by ripping off the top of a mountain and hurling it at the sound of the taunting voice. The huge piece of stone barely missed the ship and the wave it created sent the vessel scudding back toward shore. The men begged Odysseus to remain silent, but he couldn't resist calling out to the Cyclops again.

Odysseus escapes from the cave of Polyphemus,
beneath the belly of a ram.

"Hear me, you cruel and brutal one. If anyone asks you who robbed you of your eye and left you in helpless blindness, then tell them that it was Odysseus, sacker of cities, who calls Ithaca his home."

In response, Polyphemus prayed to Poseidon. "Hear me, my father, and grant my wish. If Odysseus is ever allowed to return home, let him arrive alone like a beggar and find trouble in his household."

The Cyclops tore off another stone crag and hurled it. The boulder missed the ship and this time the wave it created carried Odysseus' ship back to where his other ships waited. But Poseidon had heard Polyphemus' prayer and accepted it. The god of the sea was to remain Odysseus' bitter enemy for many years.

In the hall of King Alcinous, no one stirred as Odysseus paused to refresh himself with a goblet of wine. The Phaeacians waited with eager politeness for the Ithacan to resume his story. Odysseus set down his goblet and continued his tale.

From the land of the Cyclopes, Odysseus sailed his ships south. They came at last to the island where lived Aeolus, the divine Guardian of the Winds. For a month Aeolus entertained and feasted his guests, asking them all about the events at Troy. When it came time for Odysseus to depart, Aeolus gave him a precious gift: a bag which contained all the winds of the world except the gentle west wind. As long as the bag remained closed, the west wind alone would blow and carry Odysseus and his companions back to their home.

For nine days and nine nights, Odysseus steered the fleet, refusing to rest or sleep. On the tenth day, Odysseus saw the smoke rising from the hearth-fires of his beloved Ithaca. A deep slumber overcame him. While Odysseus slept, his men inspected the bag which Aeolus had given their captain. They were convinced that it contained gold or jewels or treasure. When they opened the bag the least bit, all the winds of the earth came roaring and rushing out. Odysseus awoke and saw in despair what had occurred. He had been so close to his home that he was nearly overwhelmed as he watched Ithaca disappear beneath the horizon. For an instant he contemplated throwing himself overboard but immediately dismissed that thought as unworthy of him.

When the winds settled, the fleet found itself back at the

island of Aeolus. With a great deal of embarrassment, Odysseus asked the Guardian of the Winds to assist him again.

"Out of my sight, you unhappy man," replied Aeolus. "Surely one of the gods must hate you if you have been forced back here. I will help you no more."

Odysseus returned sadly to his ships. For six days and nights they sailed. On the seventh day they came upon the fortified harbor of Lamos. All of the ships entered the harbor except for Odysseus' which he anchored just outside. Unknowingly they had come to the land of the giant and savage Laestrygonians. Antiphates, their king, ate the first of Odysseus' men to step ashore. He then raised a horrible cry and summoned others of his monstrous tribe. The giants came swarming from all directions and began pelting the fleet with boulders. They smashed all the ships in the harbor and speared the swimming men to eat in their ghastly feasts. Only Odysseus and the men on his ship managed to escape the slaughter and sail on, sick with grief and horror at the ungodly spectacle they had just witnessed.

III.

The solitary ship sailed on through uncharted seas. When they at last sighted land and pulled their vessel ashore, Odysseus and his companions were nearly dead from hunger and exhaustion. While his men moaned in weariness and sorrow next to their ship, Odysseus took up his spear and began to explore inland. He had not walked far when he noticed smoke rising from some dwelling in the forest. While he considered whether to approach the strange house, a large stag with great antlers sprang across his path. Odysseus skillfully cast his spear and brought the animal down. Shouldering the beast, Odysseus staggered beneath its weight back to his ship. The men rejoiced at the sight of their captain and his prize. In a moment fires were lit and the stag was butchered and set to roast. Long into the night the wanderers raised their spirits by feasting on the delicious meat.

When dawn appeared, Odysseus roused his companions and

told them of the palace he had seen in the forest. None of the men was eager to visit the palace, remembering with sorrow their encounters with the Cyclops and the Laestrygonians. Odysseus convinced them, however, that they had no choice. He divided his company into two divisions of twenty-two men each, assigning one to himself and the other to his lieutenant, Eurylochus. They drew lots to see which party would go to explore the dwelling in the forest. Eurylochus lost the draw and set out into the forest with his men. Odysseus and the others remained by the ship.

The search party came into a clearing where the shining palace was built. All around the dwelling were wolves and lions and other beasts which, to the men's great surprise, walked up to them and fawned and licked their hands. They heard lovely singing from within the palace and called aloud to the singer. The enchantress, Circe, appeared and invited all the men inside. Eurylochus was suspicious, however, and hid outside the palace. Circe fed the men and gave them wine which was filled with magic herbs. She touched the men with her wand, and they were instantly transformed into pigs. Circe drove them into a sty and threw them a handful of acorns to eat. Eurylochus waited a long time for some sign of his friends and then raced back to report their disappearance to Odysseus.

When he had heard Eurylochus' story, Odysseus strapped on his bronze sword and headed, all alone, into the forest. Before he reached Circe's palace he was stopped by the god Hermes.

"Odysseus, you must be careful," said the god. "This is the island of Aeae, home of Circe, a divine daughter of the Sun and a powerful magician. Her brother is Aeetes, the wicked king of Colchis. She has already turned half of your men into swine and driven them into a filthy sty. If you are to escape her enchantments you must follow my instructions carefully. First, I give you this plant, which is named 'moly' and which will protect you against Circe's drugs. Next, when the goddess touches you with her wand you must draw your sword and rush upon her as if you mean to kill her. She will be frightened and invite you to share her bed. Do not refuse her love but make her swear that she will devise no other evils against you and your followers."

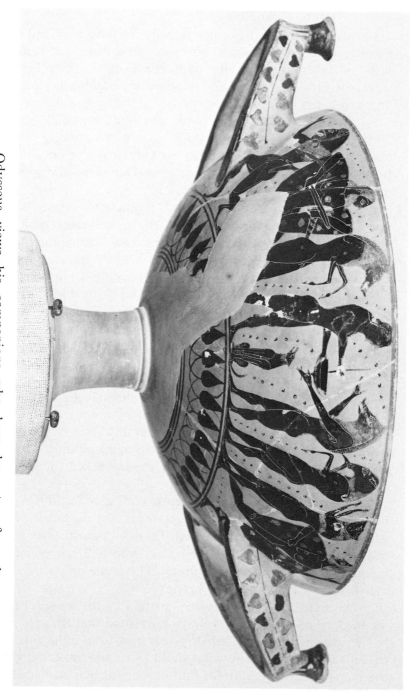

Odysseus views his companions who have been transformed into beasts by the enchantress Circe.

Odysseus thanked Hermes warmly for the advice and entered Circe's palace. She welcomed him with her drugged food and wine. But when she touched him with her wand, nothing happened. Odysseus drew his sword and made a threatening gesture. Circe dropped to her knees and screamed.

"In the name of all the gods, what man are you?" she cried. "My drugs and spells do not work on you. You have a mind that cannot be enchanted. You must be Odysseus, for only he could withstand my wiles. Come then, great Odysseus, and join me in my bed."

"Circe, I will not deny you," replied Odysseus, "but first you must swear by the river Styx, the unbreakable oath of the gods, that you will not try to harm me or my companions."

The goddess swore the oath at once. Odysseus dropped his sword and joined Circe in the delights of love, but the heart within him was heavy. After Circe had bathed and clothed him, she asked why he did not begin eating the food she had set before him.

"Goddess, how can I eat when my companions remain as pigs in your sty. Restore them to their natural forms and send for the rest of my men at the ship. Then we will all join you in your feast."

Circe did as Odysseus asked, and when all the men were restored and gathered together they held a joyous celebration in her palace. For one entire year, Odysseus and his men remained on Aeae with Circe, taking their ease and enjoying unlimited food and wine. But at the end of that time, Odysseus asked the goddess to help them return to their home.

"Brave Odysseus, you may go if you wish," said Circe, "but before you can return to Ithaca you must visit the house of Hades where the spirits of the dead dwell. There you must speak with the spirit of the dead prophet Teiresias, who will tell you how to accomplish your homeward journey. This is the only way you will ever be able to return to your home."

Odysseus and his men were terrified by the prospect of visiting the land of the dead, but they understood that the journey had to be made. Circe instructed Odysseus how to find the entrance to the kingdom of Hades and what to do when he arrived there. While the men prepared the ship for sailing, a young man named Elpenor drank too much wine and fell asleep on the roof of Circe's palace. When he awoke and saw the ship was leaving, he stumbled off the roof and fell to his death. Odysseus did not realize what had happened and sailed off to the realm of the dead.

People in all times and in all places have held beliefs concerning death. Most societies have made provision for some kind of experience after the grave. The subject has always had the terrible fascination of the unknown. Odysseus was given a rare if frightful opportunity when Circe directed him to the house of Hades. He was to see what death was like before he himself had died.

The winds carried Odysseus' ship to the very edge of the world where all was shrouded in darkness. Following Circe's instructions, Odysseus dug a pit with his sword and filled the hole with sheep's blood mixed with honey and wine. He had been told to hold off all the spirits of the dead until Teiresias had a chance to drink the offering. Before the ghosts appeared, however, the shade of Elpenor addressed Odysseus. Elpenor's ghost had not been allowed into Hades' because his body had not been properly burned and buried. The spirit begged Odysseus to return to Circe's isle and give his body a proper burial. Otherwise the ghost was condemned to wander the edges of the Underworld without ever being allowed to enter. Odysseus promised his dead comrade that he would return to Aeae and properly bury the body.

Thousands of spirits appeared from the dark regions, each wishing to drink the blood in the pit. Although he was terrified by the sight, Odysseus stood fast and refused to allow any but Teiresias to taste the blood. This was a particularly sad moment for Odysseus, for he saw among the ghosts the spirit of his own mother, Anticleia, who had been alive and well when he had left for Troy.

Finally, the soul of Teiresias approached, drank of the blood, and spoke to Odysseus.

"Great Odysseus, I know why you have come. You are seeking your home, but I tell you the search will not be an easy one. Poseidon hates you for blinding his son, and the god will make much trouble for you. But this I can tell you. You will return home if you can control yourself when you land on the island of Thrinacia. On that island are pastured the oxen of Helios, god of the sun. Whoever harms those sacred animals will never see the day of his homecoming. This is what I see in the future for you, glorious Odysseus. You will return home, but you will be alone like a beggar and find troubles in your household. Arrogant men are eating up your wealth and courting your faithful wife against her will. You may kill these men in any way you can, for they deserve a violent fate. Then you must go on another journey to a land where men do not sail ships. You will return home again. Death will find you from the sea in a peaceful manner, and you will die when you have reached a rich old age."

"Teiresias, you have been given the vision of the gods," said Odysseus, "and I thank you humbly for your information. But tell me, my lord, why will my mother's spirit not speak to me?"

"She will speak if you allow her to drink of the sacrificial blood. Any of the spirits in this place will speak if they can first taste the blood."

The ghost of the inspired prophet drifted back into the gloom.

Odysseus then allowed Anticleia's soul to approach the pit. When she had drunk, she cried aloud.

"Oh my child, what has brought you to this place of mists and dimness? Have you not returned home from Troy to your wife and son?"

"Mother, I have wandered since the day we sacked Priam's city. I was obliged to come here to consult with Teiresias. But tell me, mother, how is it that I find you here? And what of my father and my son and my beautiful wife?"

"Penelope waits with an enduring heart for your return," answered Anticleia. "But your absence was so hard on all of us. Laertes, your father, has retired to a farm away from the city and groans away his days. Telemachus has grown to be a splendid young man, although he misses you sorely. But I, sweet Odysseus, suffered most of all. My longing for you and your gentleness and your love took my life from me."

Odysseus was moved to tears by these words. As he spoke with his mother's spirit, he saw all the great queens of past ages. He saw Alcmene, the mother of Hercules, and Ariadne, the lover of Theseus. Jocasta, the mother and wife of Oedipus, and Leda,

Odysseus, guided by Hermes, consults Elpenor
in the underworld.

the mother of Helen, also appeared to him, along with many others.

When these women had departed with the spirit of Anticleia, Odysseus was met by the ghosts of his former comrades at Troy. First came Agamemnon, who had led the Greek forces. In response to Odysseus' question about his death, Agamemnon told how he had been murdered by his wife, Clytemnestra, when he returned to his home in Mycenae.

"How lucky you are, shining Odysseus," continued Agamemnon, "to have a wife like Penelope. Not only is she lovely to behold, she is faithful as well. Ah, how I long to see my son, Orestes, and how I mourn for the life which my treacherous wife took from me."

Next came the spirit of the noble Achilles, he who had been the mightiest of all the Greeks at Troy. He wore a look of extreme sadness.

"Valiant Achilles," said Odysseus, "when you were alive you were honored above all the Greeks. Even here among the dead you must command authority and respect. Do not grieve too much, my friend."

"Odysseus, do not try to ease my sorrow," replied Achilles. "I would rather be the lowliest slave on earth than king of all the dead. One day on the bright, green earth is better than an eternity in this dark, shadowy place. I have learned that life in the world, with its striving for action and accomplishment, is all that matters. Here there are no battles to be fought, no dangers to face. But tell me of my son, Neoptolemus, did he act honorably and fight bravely after my death?"

Odysseus assured Achilles that Neoptolemus had done great deeds at Troy and was a son of whom Achilles could be proud. This pleased the soul of Achilles very much and his sorrow was eased somewhat to know that his son was respected by men.

Last of all, Odysseus saw the spirit of Great Ajax standing off at a little distance, sulking.

"Great Ajax, can you not forget your anger over that armor even in death?" asked Odysseus. "Come nearer, my comrade, and let us speak to one another."

But the ghost of Great Ajax moved away without speaking, still nursing his rage that Odysseus had been given the armor of Achilles. After Odysseus had seen the horrible punishments of Tityos, Tantalus, and Sisyphus, men who had sinned against the sacred trust of the gods, he returned to his ship. His companions were only too anxious to depart from that place and they leaped to the sails and oars.

Odysseus sailed directly back to Aeae and buried the body of Elpenor, fulfilling the promise he had made to his dead comrade's spirit. Circe welcomed them and replenished their provisions of food and wine. Before Odysseus departed to continue his homeward journey, Circe alerted him to the dangers he had yet to face: the Sirens and Scylla and Charybdis. She particularly emphasized that neither he nor his men should harm the sacred oxen of the sun-god.

The ship set out, driven by a following wind across the wine-dark waters. As it neared the island of the deadly Sirens, Odysseus remembered Circe's warning. The Sirens were three sea nymphs who lived on a rocky isle in the middle of the sea. They sang to passing ships, and their song was so sweet and alluring that sailors would wreck their vessels attempting to approach too near the island. Scattered on the beach were heaps of bones, bleached white from the sun, a horrible tribute to the fatal enchantment of the Sirens' song.

Odysseus plugged with wax the ears of all his companions and told them to tie him securely to the mast of the ship. In this way the men could sail safely past the Sirens while Odysseus could listen to their song and yet be restrained from adding his bones to those on the shore. As the ship passed by the island, the Sirens began their song.

"Oh great and wise Odysseus," they sang, "bring your craft closer so that you may hear our song. Our voices are sweet, and we know everything that happened at Troy and everything that is happening now all across the wide earth. Come to us, brilliant Odysseus, and all our knowledge will be yours."

Odysseus struggled mightily against the ropes holding him to the mast and signalled to his men to release him. His companions, however, followed his earlier instructions and secured the ropes even tighter. Soon they had sailed beyond the range of the deadly voices. Odysseus' men unplugged their ears and released their captain from his bonds. Odysseus was the only man in the world to have heard the Sirens' song and survived.

The ship had two more dangers to face almost immediately. The way home to Ithaca lay through the Straits of Messina. High on the rocky cliffs on one side of the straits lived Scylla, a terrible monster with six heads attached to long necks. On the other side of the straits lived Charybdis, a creature of the sea who periodically sucked down enormous amounts of water. Any ship caught near Charybdis was doomed to destruction in the whirlpool she created. Between these two terrors Odysseus had to steer his ship.

Circe had told him to sail close by Scylla's rocks and thereby avoid the total destruction promised by Charybdis. Better to lose just six men to Scylla, the goddess had advised, than your entire ship to Charybdis. But Odysseus was not prepared to lose even six men, although Circe had told him that to fight the six-headed monster was futile. Arming himself with two long spears, Odysseus vaulted astride the prow of the ship to meet Scylla's attack. At that moment, Charybdis created a fearsome whirlpool and Odysseus' attention was directed there. Scylla immediately appeared on the cliffs, dipping her six heads down to the sea. Her six jaws each clamped shut on a sailor and the long necks withdrew up the face of the cliffs. Odysseus and his men watched in horror as Scylla devoured their six comrades.

When the ship finally cleared the straits, the men begged Odysseus to land on the nearby island of Thrinacia. They were hungry and fatigued from their ordeal and a stormy night was approaching. Odysseus reluctantly drove the ship ashore, reminding his friends of their promise not to harm the oxen that lived on the island. For an entire month, wild winds blew from the south and the east, preventing the ship from setting sail again. Their stores of food were soon exhausted, and they began to suffer greatly from hunger. The men combed the island for birds and fish to eat, but they found little to appease their sharpening appetites.

Finally, Odysseus went off alone to pray to the gods to end their ordeal. While he was gone his men, driven nearly mad with hunger, slaughtered and cooked several of the sacred oxen. When

Odysseus returned and saw what had been done, he knew that his companions had condemned themselves to death. As everyone except Odysseus feasted on the meat, Helios appealed to Zeus to punish the men for their actions. Zeus agreed.

For six days the men gorged themselves on the forbidden flesh. On the seventh day the winds abated and the men set sail from Thrinacia. They had not travelled far when Zeus brought on a violent storm and struck the ship with a thunderbolt. All of Odysseus' companions perished beneath the raging sea. Odysseus alone managed to survive by lashing together the splintered mast and keel and thus keeping himself afloat. For nine days Odysseus was carried along by the winds and the currents. On the tenth day he was washed ashore on Ogygia, the island home of Calypso. The nymph nursed him back to health and kept him on her island for seven years.

"And that, King Alcinous, is my story," said Odysseus. "After seven years I left Calypso's isle and was shipwrecked again. I swam ashore and was assisted by your daughter, Nausicaa. And that is how I came to be in the land of the Phaeacians."

Chapter *III*

Odysseus' Return to Ithaca

When Odysseus finished speaking of his wanderings, the hall of the Phaeacians was perfectly quiet. Night had fallen while Odysseus spoke and shadows played throughout the corners of the chamber. King Alcinous and his subjects were stunned to silence by the tale they had just heard. It was an extraordinary story, and the Phaeacians understood what an exceptional man this was who had endured the dangers, temptations, and sufferings of such a journey.

"Stately Odysseus, I cannot tell you how honored I am to entertain you in my house," said Alcinous at last. "Tomorrow morning my sailors will convey you back to your home. And with you will go a rich present from each of my nobles. You will return home with greater wealth than you would have brought back from Troy. This will be our tribute to your courage, endurance, and strength of mind."

Odysseus thanked his host for his generosity. The next morning Odysseus boarded ship along with a great deal of treasure. As the Phaeacians rowed with ease across the waters, Odysseus fell into a deep, dreamless, death-like sleep. The ship entered a secluded bay on the coast of Ithaca. The Phaeacians gently lifted Odysseus (who still slept) ashore and heaped his treasures around him. They reboarded thir ship and rowed home to Scheria. As they returned to their harbor,Poseidon turned their ship into stone and rooted it to the floor of the ocean. The god of the sea had been angered by the Phaeacians' willingness to help Odysseus return to his home.

When Odysseus awakened, he was not certain at first that the land he saw before him was his own. Athena disguised herself as a young shepherd and appeared to Odysseus on the beach.

"Young man," asked Odysseus, "can you tell me what country this is?"

"Of course," replied the disguised goddess, "this is the island men call Ithaca."

Odysseus rejoiced in his heart at these words. But being careful and vigilant, Odysseus did not wish to reveal his identity. He knew that there was trouble in his household, and he felt that to announce his return immediately might be imprudent. So, to fool the 'shepherd,' Odysseus began to weave an elaborate lie about his Cretan background.

Athena laughed and cast aside her disguise. "You are a devious wretch," said the goddess pleasantly. "Just as I am known among the immortals, so are you known rightly among mortals for your shrewdness, cunning, and wit. Ah, Odysseus, I admire you beyond all other men. You are so clever, so fluent in speech, and so self-possessed that I cannot help loving you and helping you."

After the goddess gave Odysseus an affectionate pat with her hand, the two busied themselves with a plan. First they hid all the great treasure in a nearby cave. Then Athena changed Odysseus' shape so that he looked like an old and miserable beggar. The glorious clothes that Queen Arete had given him were changed into filthy rags. She instructed him to go at once to the hut of the swineherd, Eumaeus, who had remained faithful to Odysseus during his long absence. Odysseus was to remain at the hut until Athena arranged to have his son, Telemachus, meet him there. The goddess told Odysseus to reveal himself to his son but to no one else. And she assured him that she would be with him when the time came for battle with the Suitors.

Odysseus went off to the hut of his old swineherd, which was located some distance from his palace. Eumaeus welcomed the old beggar who appeared at his door and made him as comfortable as he could. Odysseus spun a complicated lie for the swineherd so that Eumaeus would not guess his true identity.

Athena made her way in a flash across the water to re-join Telemachus when he returned to his ship at Pylos. The goddess resumed her disguise as Mentor and aided Odysseus' son in preparing to sail back to Ithaca. With Athena's guidance, Telemachus avoided the Suitors' ship which lay in ambush for him off the coast. He arranged to have his ship drop him off on a secluded portion of beach. Following 'Mentor's' advice, Telemachus then hiked to the hut of Eumaeus while his ship rounded the island and entered the harbor near the palace.

When Telemachus arrived at the hut, he found the swineherd entertaining an old beggar dressed in tattered clothing. Eumaeus was delighted to see the young man, and after they had exchanged greetings Telemachus sent Eumaeus off to the palace to tell Penelope that her son had arrived home safely. The swineherd departed and Telemachus turned to greet the old stranger. But the wretched beggar sat there no longer. Athena had restored Odysseus to his natural form.

"Surely this is the work of the gods," exclaimed Telemachus. "Sir, you have undergone quite a sudden change. In fact, I believe that you yourself must be one of the immortals, for I have never before seen a man like you."

"No, my son, I am not a god," said Odysseus, grasping the young man's head and kissing his brow. "I am your father, the man for whom you have grieved these many years."

Telemachus was so shocked that at first he couldn't believe that his father had actually come home.

"My son, it is not proper for you to doubt too much," said Odysseus. "I am the only Odysseus you will ever see return to you. Athena has protected me through my many sufferings and now she puts on me the shape of an old beggar so that I may observe the Suitors and plan their destruction. And you must not betray my presence in Ithaca, even to your mother, before we are ready."

Telemachus was overjoyed, and father and son joined in a long awaited embrace. They spoke of what had befallen each and then began to make their plans. They were interrupted by the return of Eumaeus from the palace. Athena was careful to change Odysseus back into the old beggar before the swineherd entered the hut.

"Telemachus, I bring you news from the city," cried Eumaeus. "While I was going to see your mother, two ships arrived in the harbor. One was the ship that brought you back from Pylos. Then a ship filled with some of those evil Suitors sailed in. You know, Telemachus, I believe those arrogant men intended to do you harm."

Odysseus and his son exchanged significant glances. Eumaeus prepared dinner; after the men had eaten and drunk their fill, they retired to sleep. The minds of Odysseus and Telemachus were filled with their plans for punishing the Suitors.

Early the next morning, Telemachus arose and walked into the city. He entered the palace and spoke briefly with Penelope about his travels. Although he longed to ease his mother's pain, the son of Odysseus did not reveal his great secret. Penelope returned to her chamber to weep for her husband, as she did nearly every day.

Late that afternoon, Eumaeus and Odysseus hiked into the city. Along the way they encountered an insolent man named Melanthius, who was a follower of the Suitors.

"You there, Eumaeus," sneered Melanthius, "why are you bringing that detestable beggar to the palace? He will only disturb the feasting of the men there. And believe me, the Suitors will not stand for it."

Melanthius finished speaking and gave Odysseus a vicious kick. Although his first impulse was to grab the man and smash him to the ground, Odysseus suffered the abuse in silence. But his heart was raging with a desire for revenge. Melanthius spoke rudely again to the two men and then entered Odysseus' palace to join the Suitors.

"Stranger, I am sorry to see you treated this way," said Eumaeus, "but these men here in the palace have no discretion nor any feeling for right behavior. If only the gods would allow my beloved master to return home, these Suitors would find a just reward for their wickedness."

As the two men entered the shining palace, Odysseus noticed an old dog lying on a pile of cow dung. The dog was covered with ticks and the signs of long neglect. Odysseus realized that the dog was Argos, his constant companion in the days before he left for Troy. Argos recognized Odysseus despite Athena's disguise and tried to raise himself from the dung heap. The dog was too old and too feeble, however, and died before he could move to greet his master. Eumaeus did not notice the dog's actions, and Odysseus wiped away a secret tear as he followed the swineherd into the great hall of the palace.

A feast was in progress, the Suitors glutting their appetites on the best animals from Odysseus' herds. When Odysseus entered the hall he circulated among the tables, begging food from the haughty Suitors. One of them, the man named Antinous, lashed out and struck Odysseus on the shoulder with a foot-stool. Only Odysseus' extraordinary self-control saved Antinous from an immediate death.

While Odysseus was thus occupied, a real beggar named Irus entered the hall. Irus had begged in the palace many times before and was angered by the presence of a competitor.

"Stranger, you would do well to get out of here," rasped Irus. "Otherwise I will be forced to use my fists to drive you from this palace."

Odysseus replied that he was harming no one. Irus continued his threats, and the Suitors were delighted by the confrontation between the two old men. Antinous suggested that the two fight to see who would be allowed to beg in the house. Odysseus was reluctant but saw that he had no choice. The Suitors gathered around the beggars, shouting in mockery and enjoying the miserable spectacle. With a single blow, Odysseus broke Irus' jaw and sent him sprawling in the dust. The Suitors roared with laughter and declared Odysseus to be the champion of beggars. They returned to their tables, calling upon Phemius, the old bard of the palace, and forcing him to sing for their entertainment.

The Suitors continued their gross and riotous feasting long into the evening. Eurymachus began to taunt and ridicule Odysseus' rags and baldness and went so far as to throw a footstool at his head. The stool missed but the incident further inflamed Odysseus' growing indignation against the Suitors. When darkness descended and the arrogant men left the palace to find their own homes, Odysseus called Telemachus aside.

"Son, we now begin our preparations," said Odysseus. "We will lock up all the armor and weapons in the house. If the Suitors ask you why you took them away, tell them that the armor had become dirty from the smoke of the cook-fires. When we are finished putting away the armor, you go to your bed and rest well. You will soon need all your strength."

Odysseus had received a message from Penelope saying that she wished to question the stranger about his journeys. She hoped that the beggar might have learned something of her long-suffering husband. After Telemachus had gone off to bed, Penelope descended from her chamber into the great hall and seated herself opposite the stranger.

"Old man, forgive my curiosity," said Penelope, "but will you tell me where you are from and what news you have gathered in your wanderings?"

Odysseus proceeded to repeat the fanciful story he had told to Eumaeus. He said that he had been born on the island of Crete and that he was the younger brother of Idomeneus, who had fought with the Greeks at Troy. He also told Penelope that long ago he had hosted Odysseus at his palace and that more recently he had heard that Odysseus would soon be returning to Ithaca.

Tears coursed down Penelope's cheeks as she wept in misery at the mention of her husband's name. Odysseus felt great pity for her suffering, but he knew the time was not right to reveal himself. He sat in silence and watched his wife's despair with unflinching eyes. It was one of the most difficult moments he had ever endured.

Penelope called in Odysseus' old nurse, Eurycleia, and asked her to refresh the stranger by washing his feet. Eurycleia fetched and filled a basin and kneeled before Odysseus. She had just begun to wash when she noticed a strange scar on the stranger's thigh. She would never have failed to recognize that scar. In wonder she stared at the man and knew him to be Odysseus. But before she could cry out, Odysseus grabbed her by the throat and spoke quickly.

"My old nurse, if you love me you will remain silent. Now is not the time for me to reveal myself. You must swear not to betray my presence before I am ready."

Eurycleia readily took the oath and contained her joy. Penelope dismissed the old beggar and retired to her chamber where she wept until sleep overtook her. Odysseus meanwhile kept watch in

Penelope and a maid at their domestic chores.

the palace and noticed which of the serving-maids sneaked away to sleep with the hated Suitors. He vowed in his heart that these faithless women would not go unpunished.

Influenced by a dream sent by Athena, Penelope arose the following morning and announced to the gathered Suitors that she had come to a decision. She would marry the man who could string Odysseus' great bow and shoot an arrow through the rings in twelve axes placed in a row. The suitors prepared for the contest by slaughtering and eating several more of the animals from Odysseus' herds. Their behavior became more and more reckless and outrageous. Ctesippus hurled an ox's hoof at Odysseus and missed. Odysseus ignored the disgraceful assault, his mind full of his plan for revenge. In the midst of the Suitors' ignoble actions, a man named Theoclymenus, whom Telemachus had brought back from Pylos, predicted that the day of Odysseus' return was near. The Suitors mocked and reviled Theoclymenus.

While Telemachus set twelve axes in a row, Penelope produced the great bow which Odysseus had left in the palace when he sailed off to Troy. She repeated her promise to marry the man who could string the bow and shoot through the axes. Telemachus took up the bow first, saying that if he succeeded in the contest all the Suitors would be forced to leave his palace. Three times Telemachus stretched the bow, and on the third he might have succeeded if he had not seen a sign from his father to desist.

"Ah, what a disgrace to me," said Telemachus, feigning disgust, "that I am such a weakling that I cannot do what my father always did with ease."

One by one, the Suitors tried and failed to string the great bow. They held it over the fire. They rubbed it with tallow. But none of them was capable of performing the deed. While the Suitors grumbled and cursed in their efforts, Odysseus drew aside Eumaeus and Philoetius, a loyal cowherd. He revealed himself as their master and asked if they would stand by him now. Each man could hardly restrain his joy, and each swore to fight to the death for Odysseus' sake. So Odysseus gave them their instructions. Eumaeus was to hand the bow to Odysseus and then lock Penelope and all the maids in their chambers. Philoetius was to bolt and lock, from the outside, the doors to the great hall.

Odysseus was nearly ready to act. He and Eumaeus returned to the Suitors and Odysseus asked to be given a chance at the bow. The Suitors were angry and indignant at this request, fearing that the old beggar just might succeed where they had failed. But Eumaeus took up the bow and brought it to his master. Odysseus handled the great bow with ease and familiarity, the way a musician would handle a fine instrument. Without the slightest strain, Odysseus strung the bow and sent an arrow whizzing through the handle-rings of the twelve axes.

The moment had come. Odysseus flung the rags from his body and leaped atop the broad stone threshold. He scattered his arrows around his feet and fit one shaft to his bowstring. His first arrow struck Antinous in the throat as that arrogant man lifted a goblet of wine. The Suitors started back in surprise and gathering fright.

"You miserable dogs," cried Odysseus, "you thought I would never return to my home and family. And so you have dishonored my household, my wife, and my son. Your behavior has shocked and disgusted the gods themselves. Now you shall pay for your sins."

A wave of fear washed over the huddled Suitors as they recognized the voice of long-suffering Odysseus.

"Oh great Odysseus, spare us," screamed Eurymachus. "Antinous was responsible for all this. He was the one who insisted we stay here and court your wife. He wished to be king of Ithaca in your place. But now you have killed him and we will re-pay you for all you have suffered."

"Eurymachus, there is nothing you can do to ease my rage," said Odysseus. "You now have a simple choice. Either fight to live or die there in the corner like cowards."

Eurymachus turned to rally the Suitors, reminding them of their overwhelming advantage in numbers. As he turned again, Odysseus drove an arrow deep into his chest and Eurymachus fell to the floor in the pains of death. The battle began.

Amphinomus rushed at Odysseus with a sharp-edged sword. But before he had taken many steps, Telemachus cast a spear and Amphinomus lay shuddering in the dust. Springing ahead, Telemachus retrieved his spear and leaped up beside his father on the threshold.

"Father, while you hold the Suitors off with your arrows, I will bring us spears and swords and armor."

Off ran Telemachus and shortly returned with the armor and weapons. But while father and son girt on their helmets and breast-plates, Melanthius sneaked into the storehouse and brought to the Suitors as many weapons as he could carry. The Suitors began to arm themselves while Melanthius ran off for a second load. Eumaeus intercepted him and struck him to the ground. With strong ropes the swineherd bound Melanthius and cast him against a column. Eumaeus and Philoetius then ran to the hall to join the fight.

A terrible struggle ensued in the great hall of the palace. Athena came to Odysseus' aid and misdirected the spear casts of the Suitors. One by one, Odysseus and his son and their two companions cut down the Suitors until the air shrieked with the cries of the dying. The walls were splattered with gore and the floor ran slippery with blood. At last, the battle was finished. Odysseus and his men stood over the heaped bodies of the one hundred and eight slaughtered Suitors.

Phemius, the bard, and Leodes, the priest, were brought before Odysseus. Leodes begged for mercy, but Odysseus knew that the diviner had joined readily the feasts of the Suitors. Leodes died under a single stroke of the sword. Phemius, however, had been forced to play and sing for the Suitors. Odysseus spared the singer of songs.

Eurycleia was summoned from the women's chambers. When the old nurse entered the hall she began to raise a cry of triumph. Odysseus restrained her (it was impious to exult over the dead), and instructed her to assemble all the maids of the palace. The women were ordered to carry the bodies out of the palace and to scrub the walls and floors of the great hall. Odysseus then told Telemachus to conduct the disloyal maids, they were twelve in number, into the courtyard and execute them. Eumaeus and Phileotius took Melanthius and punished him with a horrible death.

"Bring me flaming brimstone," Odysseus said to Eurycleia, "so that I may burn it in the hall and purify my house with fire."

Odysseus was again in command of his home. His revenge had

been savage and bloody, but he knew that he had acted in response to the will of the gods. He did not rejoice in the Suitors' deaths, although he understood that those violent men had met an appropriate fate. The brutality of Odysseus' actions had been in measure to the arrogance, treachery, and rapacity of the Suitors.

As fast as her legs would permit her, Eurycleia ascended the stairs to Penelope's chamber. With joy she informed her mistress that Odysseus was in the palace. At first, Penelope did not dare to believe the good news.

"Dear and trusted nurse, the gods must have addled your wits," said Penelope. "You know that no one would rejoice as much as I to see my beloved husband back in his palace. And yet I fear that the gods are up to some trick to increase my sorrow. Still, if some god or man has punished the Suitors as they deserved, I will go down and meet with him."

Penelope hoped desperately that the nurse was right. She had been deprived of her heart's desire for nearly twenty years and the long separation had steeled her against pain and disappointment. Like her husband, Penelope was shrewd and strong-minded. She knew that the gods could be capricious and would often fool mortals for reasons of their own. The Queen of Ithaca was perfectly self-composed as she left her chamber and descended to the great hall. But her heart pounded in anticipation.

Penelope entered the hall and seated herself by the fireplace across from Odysseus. A fire danced in the grate. Light glanced from the flames and flickered around husband and wife as they regarded one another in silence. Finally, Telemachus, standing nearby, could restrain himself no longer.

"Mother, how can you sit there with such a hard heart," the son said. "Any other woman whose husband had returned would run to him and greet him with warmth and affection. Mother, this is my father who has come home at last."

"Telemachus, you need not be excited," replied Penelope coolly. "If this is truly Odysseus, then he will know the secrets which we two alone share. We have signs by which we will know one another."

"My son, be content," said Odysseus, "and leave your

mother and me alone for a time. It would be no wonder if she did not recognize me, covered with rags and the filth of battle as I am. Go off now and begin to consider how we will defend ourselves from the kinsmen of the Suitors, for surely they will seek revenge."

Telemachus departed from the hall. Odysseus rose in silence and went to be bathed and clothed. The discreet maids of the house washed Odysseus and anointed his body with shining olive oil, throwing a beautifully woven tunic across his shoulders. Athena shed a wondrous grace about Odysseus, and as he strode back into the hall to resume his seat by the fire, he resembled the glorious gods.

"Woman, you are very strange," said Odysseus at last. "What other wife could be so stubborn as to refrain from greeting her husband? But if you will have it so, I will tell Eurycleia to make up a bed for me outside your chamber."

"I am not being strange, or stubborn, or indifferent," said Penelope. "But if *you* will have it so, I will tell Eurycleia to move from the chamber that bed you made yourself when you built this house."

Penelope was testing her husband, seeing how he would respond to her idea of moving his bed. The test worked well.

"What woman or man could put my bed in another place?" cried Odysseus in anger. "No mortal alive could accomplish that task. I built that bed into the great trunk of an olive tree which grows up through this house. I cut away the foliage and trimmed the wood and planed the trunk straight to a plumbline. I decorated and ornamented that bed with gold and silver and made it like no other bed in the world."

When Penelope heard these words her heart leaped with joy. She burst into tears and flung her arms around her husband's neck, kissing his brow.

"Do not be angry with me, Odysseus," she said. "I had to be certain. Only you could have known the secret of our bed, for no man but you has ever seen its features. Oh Odysseus, how I have longed for your return. The gods have given us so much suffering because they were jealous of our perfect happiness.

The couple held their embrace, whispering and laughing in the joy of their reunion. When they retired to their chamber and to

Odysseus' unique bed, the night was already far advanced. Athena detained the light of Dawn so that Odysseus and Penelope could enjoy the pleasures of their love. They lay in one another's arms and each told the other the story of his trials and sufferings. For the first time in nearly twenty years, Odysseus slept in contentment beside his wife, and Penelope was at peace beside her husband.

At dawn, Odysseus arose and placed upon his shoulders his gleaming armor. He instructed Telemachus, Eumaeus, and Philoetius to arm themselves as well. Odysseus realized that news of the death of the Suitors would have reached the ears of the slain men's kinsmen. He expected the fathers and brothers of the slaughtered Suitors to seek revenge. And, indeed, in the city the Suitors' blood relations were preparing themselves for battle.

Odysseus and his companions left the palace, bound for the estate where Laertes, Odysseus' aged father, had retired several years before. Upon arrival, Telemachus and the others entered the buildings to prepare a meal while Odysseus went out into the surrounding fields in search of his father. He found him working alone in an orchard. Laertes had suffered greatly because of his son's absence, and the passing years had not been kind to him. He wore a ragged and dirty tunic and his back was bent with age and toil. When his son had not returned from Troy, Laertes had retired from the city and secluded himself on this estate, tending to the humble tasks of caring for the fruit trees. When Odysseus saw his father stooped over a spade, his first impulse was to rush up and embrace him. But Odysseus restrained himself; he wished to see if his father would know him after all the years.

"I see, old sir, that you are skilled in your work," Odysseus called to his father, "and yet you do not look like one who was made for such labor. Your bearing and stature are reminiscent more of the warrior and the noble than of the farmer and the thrall. But tell me this, old one, what land have I come to? I have been seeking the island of Ithaca and its king, Odysseus. I entertained him in my house years ago and have now come to repay his visit. I am afraid, however, that I am lost."

"Friend, you have not lost your way," replied Laertes in sorrow, "but you have lost your quest. This is Ithaca, but its king, my son, has not returned to us from the wars at Troy. And I fear he shall never see his home again."

Laertes was overcome with grief and sank to the earth. He clutched fistfuls of dirt and poured them over his head. Odysseus waited no longer.

"Father, it is I, your son," cried Odysseus, grasping Laertes' arms. "Do not moan so in despair. See here, father, the scar that the boar inflicted on me when I hunted with my grandfather, Autolycus. Do you not know me, father?"

Laertes recognized the scar and knew that Odysseus stood before him. His joy was unbounded and he embraced his son.

"Father, I have killed the Suitors who infested my palace," said Odysseus. "We must act quickly to defend ourselves from the fury of their kinsmen. Telemachus and others await us at your house."

"Have no fear, my son," replied Laertes. "I will summon my servant, Dolius, and his sons. Together we shall face the challenge."

They left the orchard and returned to where the others waited. Laertes bathed himself and put on fresh clothing. When he entered the hall, Odysseus was startled by the change in his father. His back was straight and firm and the look of the old warrior had returned to his eyes. Dolius and his sons came in from the fields, and they were overjoyed to discover that Odysseus had come home at last. When they had finished their meal, they marched off to do battle.

The kinsmen of the Suitors had gathered just outside the city. Odysseus and his companions fell upon them with swords and spears and would have killed them all. Athena did not wish the bloodshed to continue, however.

"Stop the fighting, you men of Ithaca," the goddess cried in a great voice.

The men were terrified by the voice of the goddess and let fall their weapons.

"It is the will of Zeus, father of gods and men," continued Athena, "that this conflict be ended and that peace reign in Ithaca."

Thus, the killing was ended. The two sides exchanged pledges of friendship and loyalty. Odysseus reasserted himself as king; after nearly twenty years, order and prosperity returned to Ithaca.

Epilogue

The heroes of the ILIAD and the ODYSSEY share certain characteristics. They are of noble birth. They are physically strong and attractive. They are courageous and athletic.

Odysseus displays all these qualities but with a difference. He is certainly strong and brave, but most of all he is intelligent. The song with which the Sirens tempted Odysseus was an offer of knowledge. To Achilles they might have sung of battles and glory or to Paris of love and beautiful women. But to Odysseus they sing to arouse his curiosity and his need to know. Achilles and Agamemnon were great warriors, but they were temperamental and not able to restrain their passions. Odysseus never loses control of himself. Consequently, in Homer's poems, he survives while they do not.

Few, if any, figures have endured in the history of myth and literature as Odysseus has. Homer's hero is a man of such overwhelming vitality and interest that subsequent poets, playwrights, and novelists have returned to his story to find material for their own works.

The ghost of Teiresias had told Odysseus that he would not remain in Ithaca after his return but would embark on another journey. Homer chose to end the ODYSSEY with the peace treaty between Odysseus and the relatives of the Suitors. Later writers would pick up where Homer left off and compose stories about a new set of wanderings and about various adventures of Odysseus' son, Telemachus. In some of these stories, Odysseus appears in a way quite different from the way Homer had presented him.

In the fifth century B.C. (several centuries after Homer's death), the poet Pindar denounced Odysseus as an unprincipled and habitual liar. Pindar's near contemporary, Sophocles, wrote

75

several plays in which Odysseus appeared as a cowardly and depraved villain. The Latin writers of Imperial Rome (particularly Vergil and Seneca) tended to regard Odysseus as treacherous and ignoble. This is not surprising since the Romans traced their ancestry back to the defeated Trojans. These are conceptions of Odysseus very far removed from Homer's portrayal.

Dante Alighieri (1265–1321), the great poet of medieval Italy, damned Odysseus with a terrible punishment in the INFERNO. Dante's portrayal is interesting because it focuses on Odysseus as a compulsive wanderer and a seeker after forbidden knowledge. Unlike Homer's hero, Dante's Odysseus scorns the gods and his own family. He leaves Ithaca after killing the Suitors and dies while exploring regions where no other man had gone.

In "Troilus and Cressida," a play about the Trojan War, William Shakespeare (1564–1616) presents Odysseus as an eloquent speaker and a crafty politician. Two of the speeches which Odysseus delivers in the play are considered by many readers to be among the greatest lines ever written by Shakespeare.

Alfred, Lord Tennyson (1809–1892), poet laureate of Victorian England, created an Odysseus who combines the traits of the figures described by Homer, Dante, and Shakespeare. In "Ulysses" (the Latin form of the Greek name, Odysseus), Tennyson presents Odysseus as an old man nearing the time of his death. Odysseus sets sail on a journey

> To follow knowledge like a sinking star
> Beyond the utmost bound of human thought.

Tennyson's Odysseus is impassioned, restless, and defiant.

Dante and Tennyson give us an Odysseus who is on the voyage out, away from his home and family. He becomes a wanderer by choice. Homer's Odysseus, however, exerts all his energies to return to his island kingdom; he is a wanderer by necessity. In our century, the Odysseus who suffers and struggles to return to his home has made a startling reappearance in a novel entitled ULYSSES, the work of the Irish writer, James Joyce (1882–1941). Joyce was fascinated by the number and variety of Odysseus' relationships. He is Laertes' son, Penelope's husband, Telemachus' father, Circe and Calypso's lover, Athena's favorite. No other ancient hero is seen in so many different roles. In ULYSSES, Joyce creates a 20th century equivalent to Homer's Odysseus. His name is Leopold Bloom and he is a middle-aged, undistinguished man living in Dublin. At first, we might be tempted to regard the comparison between Odysseus and Bloom as ludicrous. But during his homeward journey through the dangers and temptations of the modern city, Bloom displays many of the qualities of Homer's hero. And he is, above all, Joyce said, a 'good man,' like Homer's Odysseus.

For nearly three thousand years, Odysseus has captured the imagination of each succeeding generation. Every age seems to find in his adventures a new source of interest. The Romans (some of them) hated him, and the medieval Christians were uncomfortable with his pagan piety, but no one has been indifferent to him. In the ODYSSEY, Odysseus displayed a remarkable talent for survival. He displays that talent still.

Glossary

Achilles (a kil′ez) Son of Peleus and Thetis; the greatest of the Greek warriors at Troy; slain by Paris after killing Hector.

Aeaea (ē ē′a) Circe's isle; Odysseus remained there for one year on his journey home.

Aeolus (ē ō′lus) Divine guardian of the winds; gave Odysseus a bag containing all the winds of the world except the gentle west wind.

Agamemnon (ag a mem′non) King of Mycenae and Commander-in-Chief of the Greek forces at Troy; murdered by his wife when he returned home from Troy.

Alcinous (al sin′ō us) King of the Phaeacians, father of Nausicaa; assisted Odysseus' return to Ithaca.

Anticleia (an ti klē′a) Mother of Odysseus; died of grief at the apparent loss of her son.

Antinous (an tin′ō us) The most arrogant and haughtiest of the Suitors.

Antiphates (an tif′a tez) King of the savage and cannabalistic Laestrygonians.

Aphrodite (af ro dī′tē) Goddess of Love and Beauty; ally of the Trojans.

Ares (a′rēs) God of War; ally of the Trojans.

Arete (a rē′tē) Queen of the Phaeacians and mother of Nausicaa.

Argos (ar′gos) Odysseus' faithful dog; died when he recognized his master had returned home.

Athena (a thē′na) Goddess of Wisdom and daugher of Zeus; Odysseus' patroness and protectress; ally of the Greeks.

Autolycus (o tol′i kus) Odysseus' maternal grandfather; a rogue, thief, and liar of great accomplishment.

Calypso (ka lip′sō) Nymph who rescued Odysseus from the sea; kept him with her for seven years and offered to make him immortal.

Cassandra (ka san′dra) Trojan princess who always told the truth but never was believed.

Charybdis (ka rib′dis) A sea monster who produced frightful whirlpools; one of the dangers encountered by Odysseus on his way home.

Ciconians (se ki′ni enz) Inhabitants of Thrace; Odysseus sacked their principal city, Ismarus, after he sailed from Troy.

Circe (sur′se) Enchantress who turned Odysseus' men into swine; with Hermes aid, Odysseus overcame her powers.

Demodocus (de mod′o kus) Blind bard of the Phaeacians whose songs related the events of the Trojan War.

Diomedes (dī o me′dēz) King of Aetolia; one of the greatest of the Greek warriors at Troy.

Dolius (dō′li us) A faithful servant of Laertes.

Dolon (dol′on) A Trojan spy captured and slain by Odysseus and Diomedes.

Elpenor (el pē′nor) A member of Odysseus' crew who died falling from the roof of Circe's palace.

Eumaeus (ū mē′us) A faithful swineherd who assisted Odysseus' return to Ithaca.

Eurycleia (u ri klē′a) A loyal nurse who was the first to recognize Odysseus upon his return.

Eurylochus (ū ril′o kus) Odysseus' lieutenant on the voyage home; killed by Zeus after slaughtering the oxen of Helios.

Eurymachus (ū rim′a kus) One of the principal Suitors.

Great Ajax (ā′jaks) An enormous Greek warrior who never forgave Odysseus for being awarded the armor of Achilles.

Halitherses (hal i ther′sēz) The prophet of Ithaca who said that Odysseus would not return home from Troy for twenty years.

Hector (hek′tor) Son of Priam and greatest of the Trojan warriors; killed Patroclus and was killed by Achilles.

Hecuba (hek′u ba) Wife of Priam and Queen of Troy.

Helen (hel′en) Daughter of Zeus and Leda; the most beautiful woman in the world; wife of Menelaus, lover of Paris.

Helios (hē′li os) God of the sun who kept a herd of sacred oxen on the island of Thrinacia.

Hephaestus (he fes′tus) Divine blacksmith of the gods; husband of Aphrodite.

Hermes (hur′mēz) Divine messenger of the gods; god of thieves and businessmen.

Homer (hō′mer) Blind poet who is said to have composed the ILIAD and the ODYSSEY.

Iliad (il'i ad) Homer's epic poem dealing with the Trojan War.

Irus (ī'rus) A beggar in Odysseus' palace on Ithaca.

Ithaca (ith'a ka) Odysseus' island kingdom off the west coast of the Greek mainland.

Laertes (lā ur'tēz) Odysseus' father.

Laestrygonians (les tri gō'ni anz) Cannibals who destroyed all but one of Odysseus's ships.

Laocoon (lā ok'ō on) Son of Priam who recognized the danger of the wooden horse; killed by sea serpents sent by Athena.

Lotus-Eaters (lō'tus) A tribe of people who were addicted to the lotus plant; anyone consuming the lotus lost all sense of duty and responsibility.

Melanthius (mē lan'thi us) A cruel and cowardly servant of the Suitors.

Menelaus (men e lā'us) King of Sparta; brother of Agamemnon; husband of Helen.

Mentor (men'tor) Trusted friend and advisor of Odysseus and Telemachus.

Myrmidons (mur'mi donz) The warriors who accompanied Achilles to Troy.

Nausicaa (no sik'ē a) Princess of Phaeacia who assisted Odysseus after he was washed ashore in her land.

Neoptolemus (nē op'to lē mus) Son of Achilles.

Nestor (nes'ter) Aged King of Pylos who accompanied Greeks to Troy; known for his wisdom and wise counsel.

Odysseus (ō dis'ūs; ō dis'ē us) Son of Laertes and Anticleia; King of Ithaca; husband of Penelope; father of Telemachus; the cleverest and most cunning of the ancient heroes.

Odyssey (od'i see) Homer's poem dealing with Odysseus' return to Ithaca after the Trojan War.

Ogygia (ō jij'ē a) The island paradise of the nymph Calypso.

Paris (par'is) Trojan prince whose affair with Helen ignited the Trojan war.

Patroclus (pa trō'klus) Achilles' life-long companion; killed by Hector after borrowing Achilles' armor.

Peisistratos (pī sis'tra tus) Son of Nestor who accompanied Telemachus to Sparta.

Penelope (pe nel'ō pē) Faithful wife of Odysseus and mother of Telemachus.

Phaeacians (fē ā'shunz) The people of Scheria who listened to the story of Odysseus' wanderings and assisted him to return home.

Philoetius (fi lē'shus) Loyal herdsman who helps Odysseus destroy the Suitors.

Polyphemus (pol i fē'mus) A Cyclops who was a son of Poseidon; blinded by Odysseus.

Poseidon (pō sī'don) God of the seas who hated Odysseus for blinding Polyphemus.

Priam (prī'um) King of Troy; a wise and just man.

Rhesus (rē'sus) King of Thrace; ally of Troy and owner of very special horses.

Scylla (sil'a) A six-headed monster who attacked Odysseus' crew during their journey home.

Sinon (sē'non) A Greek soldier with a great capacity for deceit; convinced the Trojans to bring the wooden horse into the city.

Sirens (sī'renz) Sea nymphs whose song lured sailors to their deaths.

Teiresias (tī r ē' si us) A blind seer whose spirit Odysseus met in the Underworld.

Telemachus (te lem'a kus) Son of Odysseus and Penelope.

Thersites (ther sī'tez) A common Greek soldier who was ugly and profane.

Thetis (thē'tis) A sea nymph; mother of Achilles.

Thrinacia (thri nā'shia) The island where Helios grazed his sacred oxen.

Troy (troi) One of the greatest cities of the ancient world; located on the coast of Asia Minor near the entrance to the Black Sea.

Tyndareus (tin dare'ē us) King of Laecedamon and step-father of Helen.

Zeus (zoos) The mightiest of the Greek gods.